A Bandit's Broken Heart

A Blood Blade Sisters Novel

A Bandit's Broken Heart

A Blood Blade Sisters Novel

Michelle McLean

Entangled Publishing, LLC
10940 S Parker Rd
Suite 327
Parker, CO 80134
rights@entangledpublishing.com

Scandalous is an imprint of Entangled Publishing, LLC.

Edited by Erin Molta
Cover design by Erin Dameron-Hil

Manufactured in the United States of America

First Edition July 2013

To TCR – my love always

Chapter One

Brynne Forrester held the plate of pie up to her chin and glanced at her daughter. "Are you ready?"

Coraline nodded eagerly, her black ringlets bouncing about her face.

"Is your napkin secure?"

Coraline gave the napkin tied about her neck a firm tug and nodded again, breaking out in a happy grin. "Ready, Momma."

"All right then. On the count of three. One…two…three!"

Brynne and Coraline dove face first into their plates, bolting the sweet berry pie down their gullets as fast as they could.

"Done! Done!" Coraline shouted, tossing her plate to the ground and jumping up to dance around her mother.

Brynne laughed and pulled her napkin from her neck, mopping up the mess from her mouth. Coraline would take a bit more work. The little girl looked like she'd bathed in berries and flaky crust. Brynne pulled her down onto her lap, wiping her daughter's face as best she could while Coraline squirmed and squealed.

"I won, Momma!"

Brynne chuckled. "You did indeed, my little chickabiddy. Now hold still so we can clean you up."

The sound of a clearing throat brought Brynne's attention to the small group of women who had stopped to observe their fun. Cora, Brynne's mother-in-law, had a strained smile on her face. The others in the group didn't try to hide their amused shock. One or two glanced about, avoiding eye contact, though most of the group stared at her in open-mouthed astonishment.

"You have a little bit of something here," Cora said, pointing a daintily gloved hand at her own chin to show Brynne where she'd missed a spot.

Brynne flushed and wiped the offending bit of sweetness from her face.

Her mother-in-law's gaze flicked to the still giggling Coraline, who Brynne narrowly managed to keep from flinging herself at her grandmother.

"I won, Gamma, I won."

"Yes, my dear, I see that," Cora said, trying to keep out of range of Coraline's sticky fingers. "But what exactly was it that you won?"

Brynne blushed, hating that the judgment glaring down from the well-connected women in front of her had erased the brief moment of levity she'd shared with her daughter.

"We were having a pie eating contest," she said, forcing a carefree tone she no longer felt.

"A what?" Cora asked, her brow wrinkling as she looked at her granddaughter.

Brynne pinned Coraline down and finished cleaning her up.

"A pie eating contest. We used to have them at the ranch. Whoever can eat a piece of pie the fastest, wins."

"Wins what?" one of the other women chimed in.

Brynne shot her a wary glance, but Mrs. Jacobs appeared genuinely interested.

"Oh, anything really. At the ranch, we'd have the contest just for fun, or we'd trade off chores or such. At the festivals in town, you could win anything from another pie to a quilt. I won a goat once."

"How…quaint," Mrs. Morey said.

Brynne stopped talking, her momentary embarrassment changing to anger at the looks of derision some of the women were giving her. Judgmental old hens. Mrs. Morey (who was connected to both the Gardner and Lowell families, thank you very much) was the worst of them. She always managed to find some fault in Brynne, no matter what the situation.

On further reflection, Brynne could admit a pie eating contest in the middle of Boston Common might not have been the best idea in the world for a picnic activity. But they had been sitting in a secluded enough spot, and they were only eating pie, for heaven's sake, not picking their teeth with their pen knives in front of the governor. Though from the women's reactions, they might as well have been.

"That sounds…lovely," Cora said.

A twinge of guilt broke through Brynne's anger at Cora's expression. The last thing she wanted to do was embarrass her mother-in-law.

"Mrs. Forrester, I was going to send this 'round to you, but as you are here," Mrs. Jacobs said, pulling a card from her bag. "I'd be very pleased if you'd join us next week for a small music soiree at my home."

Brynne took the card, touched that the woman not only thought to invite her but had the backbone to do it in front of Mrs. Morey. Though the thought of venturing into one of the social soirees made Brynne's normally stout stomach quiver in unpleasant ways.

"That's very kind of you, Mrs. Jacobs."

Mrs. Jacobs smiled kindly, ignoring Mrs. Morey's haughty sniff.

"I hope to see you there."

Brynne nodded. The women excused themselves, some more politely than others.

"Well, my dears, are you ready to return home?" Cora asked.

Coraline stuck her bottom lip out, preparing to pout, but Brynne gave her a stern look. "I actually have a few errands to run. But it would be a help if you could take Coraline."

"Of course." Cora held her hand out to her granddaughter. Coraline giggled and ran to her grandmother. Brynne swallowed past the sudden lump in her throat. It was a joy to see Coraline get on so well with her husband Jake's family. Since their daughter would never know her father, it was a blessing that she would get to know his parents.

Brynne stood and brushed at her skirts, hoping there were no lingering bits of pie anywhere on her person. Cora's man began to clean up the remnants of their picnic, and Brynne gathered her reticule and pulled her daughter in for a kiss.

"You be a good girl for your granny."

"Oh, dear girl, please. Grandmother, or even Gran if you must. But not *granny*."

Brynne gave Cora a quick kiss on her cheek. "I won't be but two shakes of a tick's tail."

"Oh. Yes, well, fine. Take your time, dear."

Brynne waved as Coraline scampered off after her grandmother, and then turned and headed toward the carriage she had waiting a short distance away. She kept her head high as she walked past the groups of people scattered throughout the park. Some still stared, a few tittered behind their gloved hands, while others flat out turned up their noses.

Perhaps the park hadn't been the best choice of locations

for a pie eating contest, but it had seemed harmless enough. And Brynne and Coraline had both needed to cut loose for a moment and have a little fun. Boston had been a haven of sorts when they'd moved here, but there were a lot of things that Brynne missed about home.

Ah well. She had other matters to attend to. She would have to save the nostalgia for later.

. . .

Brynne froze at the sound of footsteps coming up the lane, her heart pounding in her chest. For once, she was thankful for the voluminous skirts she'd begun wearing since she'd moved to Boston. They could hide all manner of things in their depths. Including the box she'd been about to leave on the stoop where she stood.

The footsteps faded, heading off in the other direction. She breathed a sigh of relief but waited for a few moments to be sure. Another quick look up and down the deserted lane with its small shops and tenements assured her she wouldn't be seen. Brynne swished her skirts away from the large parcel she'd been standing over and nudged it closer to the door of a large family she'd seen in the marketplace a few days earlier. She plucked a rose from her hat, tucked it into the string wrapped about the package, and departed as quickly as she could without drawing attention to herself.

Brynne's driver waited with the carriage around the corner and she hastened inside. As soon as the carriage lurched into action, she settled back against the seats, a small smile gracing her lips as her heart rate gradually returned to normal. She regretted having to use a rose as her calling card. A red California poppy would have been preferable, but impossible to find in Boston, especially so close to winter. Blood Blade had always left a red poppy. But Brynne would have to make do with what she had.

It felt good to be helping people again. The family she'd left the package for had several small children, all inadequately dressed for the encroaching cold weather, all thinner than they should be. Brynne had discreetly followed the harried mother until she'd found their home. She hoped her package of shoes, food stuffs, and the small bag of coins would ease their lot a bit. Helping in secret gave her the little taste of the excitement that she used to experience when she had ridden the trails with her sisters under the guise of the bandit Blood Blade.

Of course, things were very different now. She and her sisters no longer had to steal in order to help the unfortunates who depended on them. Thanks to their very profitable gold mine, they'd never have to steal again. And Brynne was thousands of miles away in the very civilized city of Boston.

Yet, despite Boston's wealth and culture, Brynne still found those who needed help. And while Blood Blade would probably never "ride" again, Brynne could certainly do what she could to alleviate suffering when she saw it.

She had her driver drop her near her favorite eating house. As soon as her cocoa arrived, she settled back with a sigh.

The anonymous gifts she'd been leaving about the city had been noticed enough that a story had appeared in last week's paper. Brynne enjoyed reading the blurbs about them. Enjoyed even more reading about how much they had helped those who had received them. Being the secret donor somewhat relieved the restlessness that plagued her, but it could hardly compare to her wild days with her sisters. And bringing happiness to others went a little way toward filling the aching hole in her heart that had been left when her husband had been killed. Brynne didn't think her broken heart would ever truly mend.

Being in Boston wasn't helping as much as she'd hoped. Brynne had been many things in her former life–a rancher, a sister, a wife, a mother, a bandit–but she'd never been a social pariah before. She wasn't finding the experience enjoyable.

Well, perhaps pariah was a bit of a stretch. Her in-laws' reputation and position in social circles saved her from being completely shunned. But it didn't stop the gossip mills from running full tilt, nor did it stop the cream of the crop from grinning politely to her face and turning their noses up at her the second her back was turned.

Brynne put down her cup and turned her face to the sun, welcoming the weak warmth of the unseasonably warm day. The small restaurant was one of her favorite spots. It wasn't often that she got to enjoy being out of doors, alone with her reflections. Her well-meaning in-laws had been nothing but kind and welcoming, taking her in without hesitation when she'd shown up on their doorstep with her daughter and sister in tow after the death of her husband. But they were sticklers when it came to society's rules. Leaving the house unaccompanied was a near impossibility, and for a woman who was more used to riding the range with a bandana covering her face and taking care of herself no matter what the situation, it was a lot to get used to.

Brynne missed the freedom of being on her own, as well as the more relaxed life on the ranch. On the ranch, life had been about survival. Here, life was about one's position in society. There were a few eccentrics, to be sure, more than Brynne had expected. But being an odd stick was only acceptable if you belonged to the right family, had the right connections, or had enough money to make everyone forget everything else.

Brynne had the money all right, but her background was a bit hazy (and she wanted to keep it that way) and the only connections she had were her in-laws. Granted, it was a good connection. Being the widow of the eldest Forrester son had opened a few doors, at least a crack, that would have been slammed in her face in other circumstances.

The waiter came back to refill her cocoa. It was a terrible indulgence, but Brynne couldn't give it up. She'd never tasted hot chocolate before moving to Boston and it had become something of a guilty pleasure.

"Thank you, Walter," she said, smiling up at the waiter. She'd gotten to know most of the staff fairly well during her daily visits and Walter was one of her particular favorites. He always brought her a little extra goodie.

He nodded and then hovered for a moment. "What is it, Walter?"

"Forgive me, ma'am, but I was wondering if you was still needing staff for your new home."

"Yes, I am," she answered, hoping he might have a good lead or two for her.

Unfortunately, her tenuous hold on propriety hadn't helped her replace the staff she needed for the house. Nearly all of the old staff had followed the previous owners to their new home. Not surprising, really, considering that the new owners had stayed in town and servants who had been with their families for years tended to be loyal. At least the good ones.

Still, of the few who had chosen to remain, only Mrs. Krause, the housekeeper, would pass Brynne's mother-in-law's muster. There was also Old Mr. Cotton, the former butler. When Brynne said old, she wasn't exaggerating. The man had to be eighty, at least. No longer really fit to fulfill his duties, but Brynne could hardly turn the man out. However, she'd put out an advertisement for a replacement for him. She needed a butler who could actually run the household. Perhaps Mr. Cotton could be a sort of advisor. Most likely he would be content enough to sit by the fire in the kitchen and doze.

"Did you know someone looking for employment?"

"Yes, ma'am," Walter said with a smile. "My little brother, Charlie. He's real good with horses. He'd make a good footman or stable boy if you have any need of someone like that."

"I do indeed." Brynne smiled, her mood considerably lighter. "The renovations are finally complete and I'll be needing the staff in place shortly. Why don't you send him along and we'll see how he works out."

Walter jotted down the address she gave him. "Thank you, ma'am. He'll be excited when I tell him." He gave her a little bow and went back to work with a grin.

At least that was one position she could check off the list. If Charlie was half as likeable as his brother, they should have no problems. As for the other staff...Brynne pondered the pathetically small group of men who had responded for the butler position. She would scrap it all and run the house herself, but she knew her mother-in-law would never allow that. If Brynne was going to live on her own, she needed a properly staffed household.

Truth to tell, she'd need one more for efficiency's sake than for propriety. Her new home was a far cry from the ranch house she'd grown up in. She'd need a full staff to keep the place from crumbling like a broken fence in a stampede beneath her feet.

"Ah, Mrs. Forrester. Imagine running into you twice in the same day."

Brynne suppressed an eye roll and tacked on a grin. She would bet her best steer that Mrs. Morey would rather be force-fed a rattlesnake than run into Brynne even once, let alone twice, in the same day. Still, it wouldn't do to be impolite. "Mrs. Morey, how nice to see you."

Mrs. Morey smirked and looked around. "Are you here alone?"

"Yes."

The woman's face puckered like she'd sucked on a lemon and Brynne held her breath to keep any of her thoughts from showing on her face. Honestly, it wasn't as if she were the only woman who walked about town on her own. Granted, she wasn't in the most fashionable area in the city, but it suited her.

Still, Brynne had no fears of being on her own. She knew how to handle herself. And anything she couldn't handle, the gun in her handbag would take care of for her. It wouldn't be the first time she'd had to shoot someone. Wandering about the streets of Boston was probably one of the safest pastimes in which Brynne had ever engaged. Not that Mrs. Morey needed to know any of that.

"Are *you* alone?" she asked, not seeing anyone with the irritating woman.

"Heavens no," Mrs. Morey replied, her hand fluttering to her chest in shock at such a suggestion. "Billy is across the street picking up a few items for me, and Mrs. Kendler and her daughters will be joining me shortly. They've been volunteering their time at Dr. Oliver's clinic. The man is a true saint." She leaned in as if she had some great secret. "He treats all the poor unfortunates in the area, often without pay."

Brynne widened her eyes, hoping that would be enough of a surprised "you don't say" reaction for Mrs. Morey. If the woman knew what Brynne had done in the name of charity, she would probably collapse right there in the street. That brought a smile to Brynne's lips and she quickly dabbed at her mouth with her handkerchief. As tempting as the idea was, spilling all the details of her outlaw past would hardly help gain her any headway in the elite circles.

"Oh my. Mrs. Kendler and her daughter are absolute angels to spend their charitable hours assisting him." Brynne hoped her sarcasm wasn't too apparent.

Mrs. Morey didn't pick up on it. "They are indeed."

Brynne almost snorted, but managed to turn the sound into a sneeze. From what Brynne had heard, the saintly Richard Oliver was a rather handsome man and fairly well off. She'd be willing to bet the pearl-handled knife in her boot that the Kendler women's charity had more to do with garnering some favorable attention from the good doctor than any true desire to help those less fortunate than themselves.

"Ah, here they are."

A dour, plump little woman strode purposefully toward Mrs. Morey, her equally dour daughters in tow behind her, and a houseboy and maid in tow behind them. Brynne didn't care what was considered proper or even safe; she'd never gallivant about town with an entire entourage traipsing at her heels.

Mrs. Kendler greeted Mrs. Morey as if she hadn't seen her in ages and then turned to Brynne, her good mood immediately fading. She gave Brynne the barest of nods.

Brynne was tempted to ignore the woman altogether, but that would be unforgivably rude and Brynne had no desire to bring any consequences down on her mother-in-law. Or on her sister, Lucy, who needed to navigate her way through society's waters as well. So Brynne forced a smile.

"Would you ladies care to join me?" she asked.

"No. Thank you." Mrs. Kendler looked down her nose at Brynne. "We have an appointment to keep and should really be on our way."

Mrs. Morey wasn't quick enough (or smart enough) to hide her surprise, which left Brynne with no doubt that the supposed appointment was a convenient excuse to save themselves from her undesirable company. Brynne steeled her face into a bland expression, hiding the surprising sting that knowledge brought. She'd never give the woman the satisfaction of knowing how effective her barbs were.

"Well, perhaps another time then."

"Perhaps." Mrs. Kendler gathered her daughters and stalked off. Mrs. Morey at least had the decency to nod in Brynne's direction before she tottered off after her friend.

Brynne sat and stared at a flock of pigeons across the lane, fuming in hurt silence. It wasn't that she liked either woman or even wanted to spend any time in their company. Still.

Brynne sighed. No sense in dwelling over what she couldn't change. She knew she should probably be getting home, but she couldn't bear going back into her in-law's massive, beautiful home yet. Coraline would be going down for a nap soon, and her sister and mother-in-law had made plans to visit one of the art museums the Forresters donated to. And she would only be in the way of the workers remodeling her own home if she dropped by there again.

Brynne really needed to find something to do with her time.

An idea niggled at the back of her mind. Perhaps she could volunteer her time to help the sainted Dr. Oliver as well. After all, if the high and mighty Mrs. Kendler could spare a few moments at the clinic, Brynne could certainly do so. She had experience in medical aid and wasn't squeamish around the ill or injured, something she doubted Mrs. Kendler or her daughters could boast. Brynne could be of valuable help at his clinic. And unlike the unholy trio who had just left, she truly wanted something of value to do with her time. Something more interesting than wandering about a museum or socializing at yet another fundraiser.

Her mind made up, she gathered her belongings and went inside the café to ask for directions to the doctor's clinic.

She was helpful, hard-working, and willing to get her hands dirty. Anyone would be lucky to have her help. It was about to be Dr. Oliver's lucky day.

Chapter Two

Brynne kicked at her heavy skirts, wondering what the good people of Boston would think if she stripped right there in the street. She'd worn dresses back home, certainly, but they hadn't been nearly as constricting or as heavily layered and she had spent more time than not in a pair of her Pa's old breeches. She never thought she'd say it, but she missed her old life, no matter how difficult it had been at times.

At least, back on the ranch she'd had something to do other than sit around gossiping with the women from her mother-in-law's society clubs or shopping for yet another dress she'd only wear once. On the ranch, Brynne might have woken every morning to a list of chores a mile long and gone to bed every night exhausted, but at least her life had had purpose.

Well, hopefully she could do something to get a little of that back. If she could find Dr. Oliver's clinic, that is. She'd already turned down two wrong streets and had had to backtrack. At last, she turned down a lane and spotted a large plot where builders worked on renovating a damaged, old building. The clinic should be just up the lane a ways.

It had been established in an old, stately home in what had probably once been a fashionable neighborhood. Now, most of the homes had been torn down or converted for other uses. Men scurried to and fro over a stone wall like ants on a picnic lunch while others shored up the support beams leaning against the wall. Brynne repressed a shudder. The thought of being so high off the ground made her head swim and her stomach revolt.

She put her head down and continued on. Brynne came to a halt in front of the clinic's gates. It still retained some illusions of grandeur. A few trees stood watch in front. A beautifully swirling wrought-iron fence covered in flowering ivy admitted entrance to a carefully landscaped yard and wide stone steps led to the covered porch of the building.

Brynne mounted the steps, hoping she wouldn't be sent away before she'd even had a chance to plead her case. She wasn't a trained nurse and had never worked in a medical facility, so they certainly had every reason to turn her away. Which was why she had come to this clinic instead of going to Massachusetts General Hospital. Hopefully, a smaller, less formal establishment would have need or some appreciation of skilled help, even if it wasn't professional.

Brynne wasn't sure if she should knock or simply enter. Thankfully, she didn't have to decide as the door opened as she reached for the handle. A kind old gentleman held the door open for her as he tipped his hat.

"Thank you," Brynne murmured, stepping inside the brightly lit interior.

The heavy drapes had been pulled open, allowing daylight to stream through the numerous windows. What had once been a grand entrance hall had been set up as an admittance ward. Several comfortable looking chairs were arranged in one corner, many of them occupied with waiting patients. A mother with a runny-nosed child; a dock worker whose arm had been bandaged and placed in a sling; an older couple who looked perfectly fine except for the cane in the man's hand. All stared at Brynne with unabashed curiosity. With her fine morning dress trimmed in ribbons and fringe, her veiled hat and soft kid gloves, she stuck out in this place like a lemon among a bushel of apples. And she seemed about as welcome.

She straightened her shoulders and marched up to a crabby-looking woman sitting behind the large desk that guarded the main staircase. The woman didn't look up. Brynne waited a moment and when the woman continued to ignore her, Brynne cleared her throat. The woman glanced up, not bothering to conceal her irritation at having been interrupted by someone the likes of her.

"Can I help you?" the woman asked. She sounded like the only thing she'd like to help Brynne with was finding a nice, high cliff to jump off.

"Yes, I'd like to speak to the administrator in charge please."

The woman's frown deepened. "Do you have an appointment?"

"No."

"Are you one of our patrons?"

"No, but—"

"I'm sorry. Dr. Oliver is a very busy man. If you'd care to make an appointment you can come back another day."

The woman put her head down and went back to her task. Brynne refused to be dismissed so lightly and had no issue with letting the woman know it. She opened her mouth to giving her lungs a good airing out but was distracted when a door opened and a man's laughter floated through the hall.

"You take care of that hand now," the man said, ruffling the hair of a small child who was gingerly holding a hand wrapped in white bandages.

"Thank you, Dr. Oliver," the mother said, giving the doctor a grateful smile.

"My pleasure, Mrs. Patrick. Keep the little scoundrel away from his papa's forge for a few more years, eh?"

The mother nodded with a sheepish grin and escorted her son out the door. Dr. Oliver looked up and caught sight of Brynne. He turned his charming smile on her and came in her direction.

Brynne stared, completely taken aback by the man walking toward her. *This* was Dr. Oliver? She wasn't sure what she had expected, but the handsome man in front her was certainly not it. He was so *young*. She had expected someone with at least some gray at his temples, maybe even a distinguished elderly man in a white coat.

But *this* man couldn't be more than thirty. His blond hair didn't have a touch of gray and his face was smooth except for the slight crinkles around his blue eyes when he laughed. As he was doing right now. An action which also revealed the dimple in his left cheek. Adorable wasn't a word she usually used to describe a full grown man, but in his case…

Brynne jerked to attention, belatedly realizing the man was speaking, and tried to pull herself together. What on earth was wrong with her? It was like she'd never seen a handsome man before. She had to admit, she hadn't seen many who could rival the good doctor. Even Jake…

At the memory of her late husband, all thoughts of the doctor's good looks evaporated.

"What can I help you with, Miss…?"

"Mrs. Forrester," Brynne stated firmly.

Was that disappointment in his eyes? Brynne dismissed the thought. Of course it wasn't. And even if it was, it was of no concern to her.

"What can I do for you, Mrs. Forrester?"

"I was hoping I could speak with you. I know you are very

busy, but it would only take a moment."

"Of course. I was about to take a short break anyway."

He took her elbow and steered her toward the back of the hall. "Mrs. Birch, I'll be in my office if there are any emergencies."

Brynne glanced back and barely kept herself from cringing at the look on the woman's face. The old bat had a chip on her shoulder the size of a house, one Brynne would dearly love to knock off for her. But that was no way to treat a potential coworker. So, Brynne refrained from returning the woman's hateful look and followed the doctor.

He opened the door for them and allowed Brynne to enter first. It was definitely a man's office. All dark wood and leather, though with the enormous window filling the wall opposite the door, the room still managed to be light and airy. Two bookcases ran the length of the walls on either side of her, interspersed with nautical paintings and filled with books and various knick-knacks.

Dr. Oliver helped her into a plush armchair in front of his desk and took the seat next to her instead of sitting behind the desk. She found his proximity unnerving but managed to keep herself in check.

"Now, Mrs. Forrester, what can I do for you today?"

"Well, Dr. Oliver, I've come to offer my services."

His eyebrows rose at that and Brynne hurried to clarify. "My nursing services, I mean."

"Ah, I see. Are you a trained nurse?" His eyes looked her up and down, his doubt plainly stamped on his face.

"Well, no, not trained exactly. But I do have quite a lot of experience in—"

"Mrs. Forrester," Dr. Oliver got up and moved to the other side of his desk and sat down, his tone instantly changing from charming to one of dismissive annoyance. "I appreciate that you'd like to find a worthy way to spend your time, and I'm flattered that you considered our establishment, but we do have a full nursing staff already on the premises."

Brynne bristled. "Dr. Oliver, I am not some bored old biddy who has nothing better to do with her time." That wasn't entirely true, but he didn't need to know that. "I have plenty of nursing experience, even if I haven't had the actual schooling and—"

"I'm sure you have. But like I said, I'm afraid this facility has all the nursing staff it requires. Of course, we are always grateful to accept the help of affluent members of the community if you would like to volunteer your time in another capacity. We host several fundraisers every year and new patrons are always welcome. Or if you'd prefer to be more personally involved, we are always in need of bandages, blankets, clothing, and the like. If you are handy with a needle, those are always worthwhile pursuits for ladies such as yourself."

"Ladies such as myself? Dr. Oliver, if I only wanted to donate goods or money, I'd have sent a maid over with the bank note and a bundle of rags."

"And we would have been very grateful for your donation. I don't mean to be insulting, Mrs. Forrester. However, we've had many patrons over the years who seem to want to work here out of a sense of adventure or even penance and all it serves to do is cause disruption and headache. I commend your willingness to be more involved with those less fortunate than you," he said, sounding anything but complimentary, "however, I simply cannot allow the disturbance to my staff and patients simply to prove to you what I already know; that you will be as unsuited to the work as the many who have come before you. Now, if you will excuse me, my time is very limited and I must be getting back to—"

"I can do more than rip bandages and sew, Dr. Oliver. If you'd give me a chance—"

"This is a medical clinic, Mrs. Forrester," he said, his face growing more rigid with every word. "All manner of disease, injury, and pestilence walk through that door. I mean no insult, but women such as you are simply not bred to—"

Brynne rose, her patience for his unjust and insulting arrogance at an end. "Dr. Oliver, I am not some sort of animal that has been "bred" to do anything. And you have no idea who I am or what manner of woman I am. That you would presume to—"

He rose as well. "As I was saying, this is not the type of establishment that a woman such as you would want to spend her time. Surely your husband—"

"My husband is dead."

Dr. Oliver stopped at that, the irritation fading from his face. "I am sorry to hear that, Mrs. Forrester. Truly."

"But you still don't think I have anything to offer you or your clinic."

"Again, I am sorry, but as I said…"

"Yes. As you said. You're as small-minded and pig-headed as the rest of the men in this city."

Dr. Oliver's eyes widened and he opened his mouth to speak but didn't seem to be able to find anything to say. Well, at least she could take some small satisfaction from their disastrous meeting. She'd rendered the arrogant bastard speechless. Hurrah!

She went to the door, grabbing the handle before he'd gathered himself enough to move. "I'll see myself out, thank you very much."

She left before he could say another word.

• • •

Brynne pushed her way through the gates and marched down the street, still fuming over her dismissal. A loud noise echoed through the air, stopping her dead in her tracks. She cocked her head, trying to figure out what had made such a sound. A moment passed, but she heard nothing else. Then a sharp crack splintered the silence, followed by an ominous rumble.

The screaming began as the rumbling turned into a deafening, ground-shaking cacophony of sound.

Brynne turned and ran back the way she'd come. She rounded the corner and ran straight into a cloud of debris and dust. Oh sweet heaven, the wall of the renovated building had collapsed.

She pulled out her handkerchief and covered her mouth, squinting to protect her eyes as much as she could from the dust. What she was able to see made her stomach drop into her toes. Bodies lay everywhere. Most, thankfully, were still moving. Men scrambled to get as far from the toppled wall as they could, crawling if they couldn't walk. Dr. Oliver and his staff were already swarming over the scene, helping those who were pulled from the rubble.

Brynne debated finding the doctor and offering her help, but the scene was one of pure chaos. And she was going to help anyway, so asking him for permission would really be an unnecessary interruption. Besides, she doubted her assistance would be any more welcome now than it had been minutes before. But she didn't see any reason the injured men should be denied her help simply because the doctor wasn't intelligent enough to utilize a good resource when it was offered.

The nurses were separating the injured into two groups; those who were injured, but still mobile, and those that were hurt more grievously and needed to be carried into the clinic. Brynne started with the man closest to her, inspecting his injuries and directing him to the group with minor injuries before moving on to the next man. She'd sent six men in that direction before she found one that was going to need help, and quickly.

She dropped to her knees next to him so she could get a closer look at his injuries. But before she could do anything, someone grabbed her arm and pulled her up.

"Mrs. Forrester? What in the world are you doing here?"

Brynne looked into the angry face of Dr. Oliver. "I'm helping. Now remove your hand from my arm, please," she said, resisting the urge to yank her arm from his grip.

He released her. "This is no place for you, Mrs. Forrester. You will be in the way and in danger here. I must ask you to leave. For your own safety."

Brynne bit back the retort on her tongue. Now was not the time or place to re-educate the arrogant bastard, even if he desperately needed someone to put him in his place. Anything Brynne had been going to say was interrupted when the man at their feet moaned and shifted, revealing an enormous pool of blood that was quickly spreading.

Brynne gasped and dropped to her knees, ignoring the doctor's shouts of protest as he dropped down beside her.

The blood looked like it was coming from the man's arm, but Brynne couldn't see the injury through his clothes. She grasped the man's torn sleeve and yanked hard, ripping it clean off. Dr. Oliver looked at her in surprise but turned his attention back to the injured man who had a gash on his arm that was pumping blood out at an alarming rate.

The man whimpered and Brynne spared a glance for him. He was hardly more than a boy. She doubted he was seventeen—if that. And he was terrified. He needed to calm down. His accelerated heart rate was only serving to pump the blood out of his body faster.

"Hi there," Brynne said, trying to make her voice as soothing as possible. He turned his frightened gaze to her and she gave him the most reassuring smile she could muster. "You're going to be fine, all right? But I need you to try and calm down for me."

The man nodded, but his breathing didn't slow. And neither did the blood. It didn't help matters that Dr. Oliver was bellowing like a constipated mule for someone to bring him a stretcher and bandages.

Brynne shot the doctor a scathing look but turned to the injured man again. "Look at me, okay? Right here," she said, pointing at her eyes.

The man obeyed her and she smiled at him. "There you go." She fumbled with the hem of her dress and grasped her petticoat.

"What are you doing?" the doctor asked, the shock clear in his voice. Brynne could picture the look on his face, but she was too busy trying to save his patient to risk a glance. She grabbed hold of the bottom of her petticoat and yanked, ripping a long length from it.

"I'm going to wrap this around your arm. You keep right on looking at me," she told the psatient.

Brynne went to wrap the bandage around his wound to form a tourniquet, but the doctor took it from her. Brynne took her eyes from her patient for a second and looked at the doctor. His face had softened. He gazed at her, almost bewildered, but at least he wasn't trying to shove her out of the way anymore. He took the makeshift bandage and started to bind the man's arm.

Brynne took the wounded man's hand in her own. He whimpered again and she murmured soothingly to him. "What's your name?"

"Edward," he said. His voice was barely audible.

"Edward, that is my father-in-law's name also. A good, strong name. Is it a family name?"

Edward nodded. "My father's name."

Dr. Oliver had finished binding his arm and motioned to some men passing by with a stretcher.

"Edward, Dr. Oliver is going to get you taken care of, all

right? They need to take you inside the clinic."

"Will you come, too?"

Brynne glanced at the doctor who nodded with no hesitation this time, although his brow was still drawn in perplexed wrinkles as he regarded her.

"Yes, of course. I'll be right here. Ready?"

Edward nodded again and the men quickly transferred him onto the stretcher and carried him through the rubble into the clinic.

Brynne stayed right on the doctor's heels and when there were no available nurses to assist him in stitching Edward's arm, Brynne scrubbed her hands and did the best she could to help. The doctor managed to get the bleeding to slow and he repaired what damage he could inside the wound and stitched it up. Edward had long since fainted from the pain, which was a blessing.

He'd begun to dress and bind the wound when a shout drew his attention.

"Dr. Oliver!"

The doctor looked in the direction of the shouting nurse and swore under his breath. She and two other nurses where trying to hold down a patient with a head wound who was convulsing.

Dr. Oliver placed a wad of bandages over Edward's wound and put Brynne's hands on top. "Bind this as best you can for now. I'll be back as soon as I can."

Brynne nodded and carefully wrapped the bandage around Edward's arm. The movement caused Edward to whimper but he didn't fully wake. Brynne looked at the rest of his arm. His shoulder had a huge bruise that was coloring nicely, and one of his fingers was definitely broken. Brynne gently probed his shoulder and Edward moaned again.

"Dr. Oliver," she called. Edward's finger needed to be splinted and his shoulder was dislocated. Resetting both the finger and joint would be better done while Edward was still unconscious.

Dr. Oliver glanced up but immediately turned his attention to stitching the bleeding gash of the patient before him.

After several minutes it became clear the doctor wasn't coming back soon. Brynne bit her lip. She knew what to do. It certainly wouldn't be the first broken bone or dislocated joint she'd set, and in far worse conditions than her present surroundings. In fact, her sister Cilla had received similar injuries when she'd been thrown from a horse when they were younger.

Brynne looked around. Everyone was scurrying to and fro, their attention focused elsewhere. Edward moaned again.

"Oh for heaven's sake," Brynne muttered.

She took Edward's forearm in one hand, placed her other on his shoulder, set her feet, and pulled with a quick, hard yank. Edward jerked with a groan as his joint popped back into place, but he didn't wake. Brynne went to work on splinting his finger.

Dr. Oliver returned right as she was finishing.

"Mrs. Forrester! How dare yo—"

"Shhh." Brynne shushed him, shooting him a furious glare. If he woke the poor boy when she'd tried so hard to keep him asleep through the whole procedure she'd brain him with a bedpan.

The doctor sputtered, his face bright red with anger. Until he looked at his patient's arm. His stitches had been dressed and neatly bound, the swelling at his shoulder had already reduced, and his broken finger lay, swollen but straight, between the others. Brynne felt a small rush of pride. She did damn fine work, if she did say so herself.

"Excuse me," she said, elbowing the doctor out of the way so she could finish binding Edward's finger to the small splint she'd found.

Dr. Oliver stepped back with a bemused expression on his face and let her finish up.

"All right then," she said when she'd finished. "Did you have something to say to me?"

The doctor's lips pursed in a mixture of exasperation and amusement. "Let's see to the others. Then we can speak in my office."

Brynne nodded, tamping down the rush of adrenaline flooding through her system. She hadn't felt this alive and useful since she'd arrived in Boston. She wasn't sure how much of the feeling was stemming from helping Edward or from the upcoming confrontation with the doctor. The possibility that it might be the latter dampened the sensation a bit.

By the time Edward was peacefully resting, Dr. Oliver's face had lost a bit of the irritated and confused look, and by the time they'd made the rounds to the rest of the ward during which Brynne helped bandage and clean up all manner of vile bodily fluids and messes, he'd lost it altogether. In fact, as they removed their stained aprons and washed the blood from their hands, the doctor kept glancing at her with bemused surprise. And a begrudging respect.

"What is it?" she asked him with a mild glare. "Did I miss a spot? Is there a smudge on my face?"

He grinned, and the laugh lines around his eyes made a reappearance. "No. You've surprised me, that's all. Not many people do."

"I suspect a great many women would surprise you if you'd give them half the chance."

"I'm not so sure about that. Most of the gentlewomen in Boston are just that. Gently born, gently raised. Brought up to be patrons of the arts and the city, and preside at fetes and balls and fundraisers, and run their households. Very few could handle themselves as well as you did today."

Brynne snorted. "I've field dressed bullet wounds and sewn up injuries with the needle and thread from my sewing kit. A little blood or case of the backdoor trots isn't going to make me faint."

Dr. Oliver's eyes rose and Brynne flushed. He must think she was unforgivably crass.

"You'll have to tell me about your experiences one of these days, Mrs. Forrester."

"Does that mean I'll be seeing you again, Dr. Oliver?" she asked.

His lips twitched and he rubbed his knuckle over his lips. "Why not? Why don't you come back on Monday? We can give it a trial period and see how you do."

Brynne released a breath she didn't realize she'd been holding. She told herself it was because she was so looking forward to being useful again. It had nothing to do with wanting to see the arrogant ass. Even now, after everything she'd done that morning to help, he was still only willing to let her return on a trial. Fine. She'd show him what she was capable of.

"Well then, I suppose I will see you Monday then, Dr. Oliver."

"I'll escort you home."

"That's not necessary."

"Necessary or not, I will accompany you."

Arguing further was pointless, so Brynne gathered her shawl and waited by the door.

Her heart fluttered as he strode toward her. She didn't like what the sensation might mean. She would have to be careful around the doctor.

He smiled when he reached her and her heart jumped again.

Oh, yes. Very careful.

Chapter Three

If Brynne had realized what a commotion arriving home on the arm of *the* Doctor Richard Oliver would cause, she would have been more forceful in insisting he remain at the clinic. Cora was beside herself with smug excitement. She'd been trying to get Brynne to show some interest in the eligible bachelors around town, feeling she'd been a grieving widow for too long. But Brynne wasn't ready for any of that and had told her so in no uncertain terms.

Judging from her mother-in-law's expression, being escorted home by a handsome and seemingly unattached man made Cora as pleased as a cat with his nose in a fish barrel. It was, however, a huge disappointment for the woman Cora was entertaining.

Mrs. Morey sat ramrod straight in her chair, her hands folded primly in her lap, with the most scathing look of dislike Brynne had so far seen in this fair city. The look evaporated as quickly as it had appeared, to be replaced with a smile that barely touched her lips.

Brynne was a little confused by Mrs. Morey's enmity in

this particular instance. She supposed it might have to do with running into Brynne for a *third* time that day. That might be enough to drive the poor old biddy to drink. Then again, Mrs. Morey had never needed a reason to dislike Brynne. None of the society women Brynne had attempted to socialize with had been very welcoming. Brynne was damned thrice over for committing the unpardonable sins of having been born "out in the heathen west" instead of in their fair city, for having an obscene amount of money that came from a ranch and a mine she had worked herself, and for being widowed and independent and wanting to stay that way.

Brynne had never quite understood the society mavens' disdain of her wealth. The vast majority of their families had earned their money the old fashioned way, by working for it in every industry from textiles to seafaring. Frankly, the way in which many prominent Bostonian families had made their wealth and what they chose to do with it was one of the reasons Brynne had assumed she'd fit in well.

Quite a few families had been a little less than ethical, or even legal, when it came to building their fortunes. There was more than one family in Boston who had a few fingers in the smuggling trade and rum-running, not to mention the occasional outright swindle. But, they were incredibly generous with their oft-times ill-gotten gains—patronizing museums, schools, hospitals, and many other worthy institutions. In truth, they weren't so different from a girl who'd spent a few years raiding the corrupt wealthy of the west behind the mask of a bandit in order to save her town and ranch from going under.

The Bostonian elite weren't flashy with their wealth either, and didn't seem to approve of those who were, an attitude Brynne admired. But Brynne, with her hazy background, Catholic tendencies (thanks to her housekeeper and surrogate mother, Carmen), shiny *new* money, and murdered husband, was simply too…other, wrong, outside.

Even with all that, while she hadn't been particularly accepted, she hadn't been outright shunned. Yet. The looks Mrs. Morey was throwing at her suggested she soon would be, but she couldn't imagine what horrid misstep she'd committed since earlier that day when she'd seen the old bat.

Until she noticed where Mrs. Morey's eyes were focused. On Brynne's hand, which was still looped through Dr. Oliver's crooked elbow. Brynne let go and took a small step away from the doctor. Mrs. Morey's smugly pursed lips had Brynne clenching her fists within the folds of her skirts. She had half a mind to wrap her arms around the good doctor and kiss him senseless right in front of dear old Mrs. Morey simply to prove that she wouldn't be intimidated. But Brynne would hate for her mother-in-law to suffer any repercussions because of her. Besides, it might give Dr. Oliver the wrong idea, and he had enough of those about her already.

"Richard, what a delight to see you," Cora said, coming toward the doctor with outstretched hands. She greeted him warmly and pulled him toward a sofa. "You must stay for some refreshment and tell us how you came to meet up with our dear Brynne."

"Ah, that is a tale that must be told another time, I'm afraid. I must be getting back to the clinic. I simply wanted to make sure Mrs. Forrester made it home safely."

Cora pouted prettily. "You work too hard, my boy. You need to learn to enjoy life a little more."

"Ah, no worries, my dear Mrs. Forrester, I am always sure to enjoy myself whenever time permits."

"Will we see you at the Cabot's ball on Friday?" Mrs. Morey asked, fairly oozing sickly sweet charm.

"Certainly. I wouldn't miss it." Before Mrs. Morey could reply, Richard turned to Brynne. "And will you be attending, Mrs. Forrester?"

Brynne hesitated. She hadn't planned on attending. She turned down most invitations. She preferred to stay home with Coraline than squeeze her body into an impossibly tight corset and subject herself to a room full of disapproval from which there was no escape.

Cora saved her from having to answer. "But of course, she'll be attending."

Brynne turned surprised eyes to her mother-in-law, who gave her a subtle wink. So much for politely declining.

"Excellent. I shall look forward to seeing you there." He took Brynne's hand and kissed it. "Until Friday, Mrs. Forrester."

Brynne resisted the urge to pull away from him, disengaging herself as quickly as politeness allowed. It didn't fool him, if the arrogant smirk on his lips was any indication. He tipped his hat to Mrs. Morey and excused himself.

The second the door closed behind him, Mrs. Morey pounced. "How in the world did you end up on the arm of one of the most eligible bachelors in Boston? Are you feeling a bit under the weather? Dr. Oliver is a wonderful physician, to be sure, even if his clinic is a bit of a distance from here. There are several very fine doctors who will come to you, after all, and you needn't worry about them being indiscreet, no matter what is ailing you. No need to travel all the way to Dr. Oliver to keep your malady private. I do hope it's not serious, my dear."

Her tone held a false note of friendly interest, but Brynne could see right through her. Brynne forced a smile, biting back the retort that threatened to erupt. "I am perfectly healthy, thank you Mrs. Morey. I was merely at his clinic to volunteer my services. I stayed to help when a wall collapsed at a building nearby and some men were injured."

"Oh my dear," she said, holding a handkerchief to her nose as if Brynne had been wallowing in filth. "Quite noble of you, to be sure, but spending so much time around such…unfortunates mightn't be the wisest course of action. Although, it certainly afforded you an opportunity to gain the attention of our dear doctor."

Brynne wasn't sure what the woman accused her of, but she resented the hell out of it. Cora must have sensed Brynne was reaching the limit of her patience because she jumped in before Brynne could respond.

"Well, I think it was splendid of you to help those poor injured men. I do hope it wasn't too trying for you."

"Not at all. I was glad to be of help."

"And you'll be seeing Dr. Oliver again?" Mrs. Morey asked, her expression almost daring Brynne to say yes.

"Yes. I've offered to help at the clinic on a daily basis."

Mrs. Morey laughed. "Oh my dear, what in the world could you possibly do to help? Change bedpans? Mop floors?"

Brynne's eyes narrowed further. "If that is what is asked of me, yes. I've certainly done far worse."

Mrs. Morey's amusement faded and she fixed Brynne with a withering glare. "I hope you really are doing this out of the goodness of your heart and not under any ill-conceived notions that you might gain Dr. Oliver's notice or favor by playing the saint. He's had his eye on my Elizabeth for several years now and I won't have you ruining her chances with him."

Ah. And there it was. Mrs. Morey didn't want Brynne interfering with her plans for her odious daughter. Brynne very much doubted Dr. Oliver had any interest in Elizabeth Morey. She was as mean-spirited and obnoxious as her mother and was as ugly as a mud fence. Not that Brynne had any intention of trying to take the doctor's attention away from anyone. She was only interested in working at the clinic as a way to do something meaningful with her days, not as a way to snare a new husband.

But she couldn't resist torturing Mrs. Morey a tad. "Oh," she said, feigning surprise, "I wasn't aware that Richard was

interested in any of the young ladies in town." The use of
his Christian name felt odd on her tongue and she'd never
address him so to his face, but watching Mrs. Morey try to
contain herself at Brynne's informal use of his name was
priceless. "We spoke quite extensively today and he never
mentioned your daughter."

Mrs. Morey sputtered and Brynne threw in one more
barb for good measure. "Don't you worry, Mrs. Morey. I'm
sure working in such close proximity with him every day
will in no way interfere with whatever plans he may have in
regards to your daughter."

Cora sat on the sofa, her face as blank as she could
make it, though Brynne could see how hard it was for her
mother-in-law to keep herself together. Mrs. Morey excused
herself very soon after, giving Brynne several parting glares
as she flounced out of the house and Cora relaxed against the
cushions with relief.

"Oh for heaven's sake, I feared she'd never leave. I
thought for sure she'd have a fit right here in our salon and
we'd be forced to call your dear Richard back to see to her."

Brynne's lips twitched. "He is not my *dear*. Or my *anything*.
I shouldn't have needled her or led her to believe there was
anything more between us than there is, but I couldn't help
myself. She is really worked up over this. Is he that great of a
catch?"

Cora nodded. "Every momma of every unattached girl in
the city is after the poor boy. He's charming, utterly brilliant,
and is connected to no fewer than five of the most influential
families in the city by blood or marriage and by friendship or
business to most of the rest of them. Throw in the fact that
he has more money than a bank dipped in gold and a set of
heavenly blue eyes that would make a woman twice my age
swoon, and you've got yourself the most eligible bachelor in
Boston."

Brynne sighed. All she'd wanted to do was help at the clinic and ease a little boredom, and instead, she'd somehow managed to alienate herself even further from the group of societal mommas that could make or break her reputation. For herself, she didn't care so much. But Lucy was getting older. At eighteen, she was certainly old enough to marry if she wished. The last thing Brynne wanted to do was ruin Lucy's chances at being accepted. She had a hard enough road as it was, coming from the same rough-and-tumble background as Brynne. And Coraline didn't need the stigma of a shunned mother following her for the rest of her days.

"As much as I hate to do anything that might make that old bag happy, I'll make sure she knows I don't have any designs on her darling doctor. In fact, the man is quite bothersome. I'll only deal with him as much as necessary at the clinic. His virtue is quite safe from me."

"If you say so, my dear," Cora said. She dug out her needlepoint and started stitching, a smug smile barely concealed as she bowed her head to her task.

"Cora," Brynne said, her voice full of warning.

"What?" Cora's face practically shone with angelic innocence.

Brynne considered stopping the wild schemes and dreams she was sure were floating through her mother-in-law's head, but knew it would do no good. She'd told the sweet woman a hundred times over that she had no intention of ever marrying again and Cora was equally as sure that she would. They'd come to a bit of an uneasy truce on the matter. However, Brynne had a sinking feeling that now that Cora had someone specific to set her sights on, the discussion might be revisited.

But for now, there was another subject that Brynne needed to discuss with Cora. One she'd been dreading. With the renovations of her home complete, it was time for her,

Coraline, and Lucy to move into their own place. Leaving her in-laws was proving to be more difficult than she'd anticipated. Especially when she observed how happy Coraline was here. But it was time to stop beating the devil around the stump and get it over with.

Brynne was about to speak when the sound of tiny running feet and childish giggles rang through the corridor. Both Cora and Brynne turned toward the door, alight with anticipation.

Coraline flew into the room. "Momma!"

"Hello, my little chickabiddy." Brynne scooped her up and nuzzled her neck. Coraline erupted in a shriek of giggles. Brynne watched her daughter laughing and her heart clenched. She snuggled into her, cuddling the little girl into her chest. No matter what sort of day she'd had, all it took was one moment in Coraline's company and all was right with the world again.

"She looks so much like Jake," Cora said, her voice pensive as she watched her granddaughter.

"She does," Brynne agreed, smoothing Coraline's black ringlets from her face. Coraline wiggled to get down and ran to her grandmother.

"Story! Story!"

"Why don't we have Lucy read you a story," Cora said, ringing her bell to summon one of the servants. "I think your Momma has something she needs to tell me."

Brynne looked at her mother-in-law, surprised, not for the first time, at how astute the older woman was.

Beth, Brynne's personal maid, came in and fetched Coraline, luring her away with promises of a sweet treat from the kitchens before she was taken to her aunt. Brynne smiled as they left. The whole household doted on her daughter. In fact, she and Coraline had been downright spoiled, fawned over at every turn by everyone in the Forrester's household. They'd even welcomed Lucy with open arms. Which was another reason Brynne had delayed moving into her own home.

Still, after living under her in-laws' roof for almost a year, Brynne longed for her own space again. She'd been used to being mistress of her own domain, taking care of not only her sisters, but a whole town.

She felt a sudden pang of homesickness for the Richardson ranch in California. The place where she'd grown up, met Jake, and fallen in love with him. She missed him so much sometimes she feared she'd go mad.

At least on the ranch, she'd had plenty to do to keep her occupied, keep her mind off what she'd lost. But here…here there were servants for everything. Servants who wouldn't let her help, who seemed almost offended that she wanted to do things for herself. Brynne was so stifled and bored she felt a bit cracked. She hoped having her own household would go a little ways toward alleviating that. And it would certainly provide more freedom.

The Foresters' attention bordered on oppressive, as was their determination that Brynne be accepted into Boston society. Cora meant well and did her best to let Brynne run her own life, but she didn't always understand Brynne's "quirks." Such as Brynne's need to be out in the fresh air, using her body for something more demanding than a barely breathing dress hanger. Brynne tried to squeeze a deep breath past her corset and sighed.

Well. Time to take charge of her own life again. She'd wallowed in her misery over Jake's death long enough. She couldn't hide with his family forever. It was time to start living again.

"Out with it, my dear," Cora said, her kind tone softening the sharpness of her words. She took Brynne's hand. "Your house is ready, isn't it? Has been for some time, I'd wager…"

"Yes." Brynne wasn't even surprised the older woman

knew her news. "It's not that we haven't been happy here…"

"I understand." Cora patted her hand. But her eyes stayed creased with concern.

"But…" Brynne prompted.

"Boston isn't quite as tolerant as California. You are a widow…living alone. There could be talk. I want you and Coraline to be accepted."

Brynne snorted. "I think that ship sailed long ago."

Cora gave her a good-natured scowl. "Perhaps. But there is no reason we must sink it before bringing it home again."

"I won't be alone. Lucy will be with me. And I've hired most of the staff I will need, in addition to those from the previous owners who have chosen to stay, so the household is nearly set up already. It will be perfectly respectable."

Cora didn't seem reassured.

"The house is really lovely. I can't wait to show it to you. And remember, it's very close. Just over on Cherry Hill Street, so you'll still be able to see Coraline every day."

"Yes, that is true," Cora said, a genuine smile breaking out on her face.

"In fact, I was hoping you'd agree to mind after her in the mornings, when I volunteer at Dr. Oliver's clinic."

"You'll be working with him every morning?"

Brynne narrowed her eyes. "I will be working in his clinic, not with him."

"Still, that seems a very…worthy pursuit of your time."

Brynne was going to argue, but decided she didn't have the energy to fight a battle she'd never win. Nothing she said would change Cora's mind.

"It will be wonderful to still have Coraline here every day. And I'd love to help in any other way that I can. I hope you know, my dear, if it doesn't work out, or if you'd ever like to return, this will always be your home. Always."

Brynne was surprised at the tears that pricked her eyes.

She hadn't been sure what to expect when she and Coraline had showed up on the Foresters' doorstep, with Lucy in tow to boot. Leo, Jake's brother and her sister Priscilla's husband, had written to his parents to tell them about Brynne and Coraline and apprise them of their impending arrival. But Brynne hadn't been sure what their reception would be. The Forresters had been more welcoming than Brynne had ever dared hope.

She had already stayed far longer than she had anticipated. Frankly, her mother-in-law had made it very difficult to leave. It had been a long time since Brynne had been mothered by anyone. Her own mother had died many years ago and while their housekeeper Carmen had done her best to give the girls all the mothering they needed, it wasn't the same. Bless Carmen's loving heart, but she had been more of a drill sergeant than a mother. Then again, with Brynne and her two sisters, she'd had to be.

Cora had begun to fill the hole that had been left in Brynne's heart when her mother had died. And Brynne loved being with Jake's family, in the home where he'd grown up.

"The choice of your staff is of the utmost importance," Cora said, breaking into Brynne's reverie. "You said most of the staff is already in place?"

"Yes, the cook, kitchen staff, and household maids have been retained. There were a few who'd chosen to leave, but the cook had a niece looking for a position and one of the maids had a sister…"

"Good, very good. And the housekeeper?"

"Mrs. Krause. She's agreed to stay on as well. The old butler was finding his duties a bit taxing but will stay on in another capacity, so I'll need to find a new one. I have several appointments set up already."

"A good butler is hard to come by, but I do know of one or two that are available, or can be bribed away from their current situations if your appointments don't pan out," Cora said with a conspiratorial wink.

"Perhaps I can lure Mr. Peterson away from you," Brynne teased.

"Oh, I have no doubt that you could. Or Coraline could, in any case. One bat of those beautiful little eyes and Peterson will be packing his bags and high-tailing it to Cherry Hill Street."

The staff at her in-law's had been, for the most part, welcoming and friendly. Mr. Peterson had been a tough nut to crack. He got on well with Brynne now, and adored Coraline as much as the rest of the household. But he'd disapproved of Brynne's independence and less-than-refined ways, especially her penchant for riding astride. He'd have a fair epileptic fit if he knew how she'd spent most of her time on horseback in California. If he regarded galloping through the park as scandalous, he'd never recover from the knowledge that Brynne had spent years behind a black bandana, raiding not-so-innocent victims of their ill-gotten gains as one of the notorious Blood Blade's band of thieves.

How times have changed.

"When will you be leaving?" Cora asked with a slight hitch in her voice.

"I purchased the house fully furnished, so it is really only a matter of moving our personal belongings. I thought sometime this week…"

Cora nodded. "Well, we'll miss having you here, to be sure. But I wish you much happiness in your new home."

Brynne gave her mother-in-law a hug, glad that her news had been received so well. She should have known her mother-in-law would make it easy on her. She'd been smoothing the way for Brynne ever since she'd arrived in Boston. Brynne hoped she'd be able to repay the older woman someday. Or at the very least, not let her down.

Chapter Four

Richard climbed down from the carriage and dragged himself into the clinic. It had been a miserably long day. Though, one interesting development had arisen from it. Mrs. Brynne Forrester. She was an absolute mystery. And a beautiful one at that.

When she'd shown up at his clinic, he'd assumed she was like all the other bored ladies who had wandered through his door. They all wanted to either escape from their over-indulged lives in a perhaps genuine, but misguided, attempt to walk on the dodgy side for a bit. Or they wanted to gain his favor by feigning interest in his work. Both were a huge waste of everyone's time.

But Mrs. Forrester had proven to be a surprise. She hadn't been lying when she'd said she had medical experience. How she had gained such experience was one of many things he wanted to discover about her. She looked like all the other genteel, refined ladies he knew, but he suspected there was a lot more to her smoldering under the surface, something much more wild and free than anything he'd ever come across before. His lips still twitched every time the phrase "backdoor trots" crossed his mind.

For the first time in his life, he was genuinely interested in getting to know a woman a little better. More than that. He was bound and determined to unearth all of the beautiful Mrs. Forrester's secrets.

He entered the clinic and headed straight up the stairs, dodging Mrs. Birch. He was too tired to deal with her. She had an even worse opinion of the ladies who tried to use the clinic to catch his attention than he did, and he didn't have the energy to talk her into accepting Mrs. Forrester graciously. He'd have to speak to her before Mrs. Forrester's arrival Monday or things could get ugly.

Mrs. Birch was a wonderful housekeeper and managed to keep things running smoothly at the clinic as well. And he appreciated her protectiveness toward him. But it was trying at times.

When he reached his rooms, he kicked off his shoes and stripped, tossing his clothing to his waiting butler. Of course, butler was rather a broad term for all the jobs Mr. Chasely handled. He was butler, clinic administrator, valet, and anything else Richard needed him for.

Richard kept a strange household. Four days a week, his home served as a medical clinic for the community, especially for those who were unable or unwilling to go to the hospital. He also kept a few beds for those he needed to keep an eye on. But for the most part, once clinic hours ended, it was only him and his staff in the building.

The upper floors were reserved as his private residence, and Mrs. Birch ran them with the same efficiency she ran the clinic. Everything was clean, tidy, and well organized. And heaven help the person who disrupted Mrs. Birch's tightly run ship. Richard had only just met the lovely Brynne Forrester, but he had the feeling she was the type who caused disruption wherever she went. Not through any deliberate action of her own, of course, but simply by being who she was.

Chasely scooped up the rest of Richard's clothes and draped them over his arm. "Will there be anything else tonight, sir?"

"No, Chasely, that will be all." Richard absentmindedly took a swig of the brandy that Chasely had left on his bedside table. "Actually, what can you tell me about Mrs. Brynne Forrester?"

"Oh, I suspect I know about as much as anyone, sir."

Richard doubted that. Servants tended to be insanely well informed about anything having to do with their employers, and Chasely was even more informed than most. Richard paid him well to be sure of it.

"And what does everyone know about her?"

"She's from out west, California, where she and her sisters own a ranch and a rather profitable gold mine."

Richard's eyebrows rose at that. "What of her late husband?"

"Jacob Forrester, son of Mr. Edward and Mrs. Cora Forrester."

"Was he the one who went off adventuring and never came back?"

"So to speak, sir. I believe he tried his hand at bounty hunting for a time, or some such profession. No one is quite sure how he came to know Mrs. Forrester, but his family lost all contact with him soon after he informed them of his intentions toward her. His brother, Leonardo, went out to find him and is now married to Mrs. Forrester's sister."

Well, now, that was interesting. Both Forrester boys marrying sisters. Must be quite a family.

"How did her husband die?"

"They say he was murdered, although the Forresters took care to keep the more sordid details from the papers."

"And now she lives here with the Forresters."

"The renovations on her own residence were completed recently and she's been busy retaining staff to run it. Mrs. Birch's nephew has applied for a position there."

"She'll be living there alone?" Richard was surprised. It wasn't unheard of, of course, for a widow to live alone. But since she hadn't had her own household here to start with, it was a bit odd that she'd choose to live on her own.

"Not entirely alone, no sir. Her younger sister will most likely be living with her. And her daughter, of course."

"She has a daughter?"

"Yes, sir."

A widow alone with her child, whose husband had been murdered. Who moved all the way across the country to live with in-laws she'd never met, and who was now setting up her own household. The woman had gumption, that was for certain.

Chasely said goodnight and excused himself. Richard barely heard him leave. His mind was on Mrs. Forrester. Brynne. The way her deep brown eyes flashed when he'd said something to anger her. Her determination to get her way. Her soft voice as she'd spoken to the frightened boy she'd helped with the hands of a person who was no stranger to blood and trauma. Who was this woman who had walked into his life?

Richard couldn't wait to find out.

• • •

Brynne held the letter in trembling hands, not reading it but staring at the way the letters scrawled across the page. Jake's handwriting.

She looked up at the man who had brought it to her. A man she hadn't seen in several years and never dreamed she'd see again. Mr. Finnegan Taggert sat across from her, his hat in his hands. He held himself proudly, but the way he twisted his hat around and around betrayed his nervousness. He had a right to be anxious. Brynne suspected he hadn't been well received at any of the other households in Boston.

He was handsome enough, very handsome actually. But few would see it through the tattoos that marked his face. Several lines extended from beneath his lower lip down his chin, but it was the T shaped markings under his cheekbones that had made Brynne's eyes raise when she'd first met him two years ago; and she'd been used to seeing strange people and sights.

Mr. Taggart noticed her staring and stood. "I'm sorry. I know I shouldn't have come. I'll see myself out."

"Oh no, please, Mr. Taggart," Brynne said, standing as well. "Please, stay."

Mr. Taggart took his seat again and resumed his hat twisting.

"I'm sorry, Mr. Taggart. I'm being unforgivably rude. It's only…I never thought I'd see you again, since the last time I saw you was when…when…"

"When I performed the marriage ceremony for you and Jake."

To her utter embarrassment, tears filled her eyes and raised a lump in her throat. She'd hoped she was past such moments catching her unawares. It had been so long. But the sight of Mr. Taggart brought the memory of that wedding day rushing back.

She and Jake had loved each other so much. They couldn't wait long enough for the town preacher to get back from his travels to marry them. When Mr. Taggart, an old friend of Jake's, had come calling, it had seemed like a godsend. An Irishman who had become a member of the Mohave tribe, he had offered to marry them according to Mohave custom.

They had viewed it as a type of hand fasting. They knew their union wouldn't be legal, but in their eyes, it had been binding, and the legality issue could have been taken care of when the preacher returned. Only Jake hadn't lived that long.

Lucy entered the room while Brynne was trying to compose herself. "Brynne, you must see my dress for the ball. It was just delivered, and it's the most beautiful…oh." Lucy stopped short and stared at Mr. Taggart. "I'm sorry, I didn't realize you had company."

Brynne made a supreme effort to pull herself together. "Lucy, this is Mr. Finnegan Taggart. He was a friend of Jake's. The one who married us, in fact."

Lucy's eyes grew wide and she gave Mr. Taggart a little head bob. "Pleased to meet you, Mr. Taggart."

"The pleasure is mine, Miss Lucy."

Lucy remained frozen, her gaze never leaving his face. Her fascination began stretching into ill-mannered territory and Brynne cleared her throat to get Lucy's attention. Lucy blinked, a delicate blush staining her cheeks. "I apologize, Mr. Taggart. It's been such a long time since I've seen tribal markings."

His eyebrows rose a notch. "You recognize the marks?"

"Yes. We grew up farther north than the Mohave territories, but we still met quite a few." Lucy's eyes focused on the T-shaped marks on his cheeks. "You were an important man in the tribe."

Surprise flared again in his eyes. He didn't answer for a moment and then nodded once. "At one time, yes. But that was long ago."

His tone left no room for more questions though Brynne could tell Lucy was dying to know what had happened to this man. She was curious as well. She'd only met him the once, and at the time, had been more interested in her marriage and new husband than the curious man who had bound them together. Mr. Taggart was obviously not Mohave by birth. How had he come to not only be accepted enough into their tribe to be tattooed, but to bear the markings only the most important men of the tribe wore?

Lucy still hadn't pulled her gaze from Mr. Taggart, who was returning her regard with amused interest.

"Lucy," Brynne said, "would you mind checking on my gown? Beth should be airing it out."

Lucy reluctantly turned from Mr. Taggart. "Of course."

She left the room, tossing a last gaze over her shoulder before she closed the door.

Brynne turned her attention back to the letter in her hands. "Jake speaks highly of you here." She was glad her voice broke only slightly on her late husband's name. She didn't think life without him would ever get easier, but she did hope to be able to speak of him someday without her emotions coating her words. "He never told me how the two of you met."

"Ah, well, that is quite a long story. You knew your husband's profession before he became a ranch hand on your property?"

Brynne nodded. Jake, much to his affluent Bostonian family's dismay, had longed for more adventure than a Harvard education could gain for him and had sought excitement out west. After a series of odd jobs, he had found his calling…as a bounty hunter. It was how they'd met, in fact. Jake had been after the bandit Blood Blade and his gang. He'd had no idea that the young rancher he had started working for in order to gain information was actually part of the bandit's band. A band run by Brynne's middle sister, Priscilla. By the time he'd found out, he'd been too in love with Brynne to turn her in. And once he'd understood the reasons behind their activities, he'd believed enough in their cause to join them himself.

"Were you one of the men he worked with? Or one of the

men he'd been paid to find?" Brynne asked.

Mr. Taggart actually blushed. "One of the latter, I'm afraid. The circumstances behind it were all a big misunderstanding. Once Jake knew my story, he let me go."

"You will have to tell me that story sometime, Mr. Taggart."

"Sometime," he said, a small, sad smile tugging at his lips. "Anyhow, I worked with him for a time, and once we parted ways, we kept in touch, even after I left for England. He gave me that letter to use as references should I ever be in need of employment. Which, as you are aware, I am now."

"Yes," Brynne said, reluctantly putting away the letter from her husband and pulling out Mr. Taggart's other references. "These are certainly impressive recommendations. You worked for an actual duke?"

"Yes. Truthfully, his lordship was a bit of an odd bird, even by my standards. I started out as more of an exotic addition to his collection of oddities, but I found that I was actually rather good at running his household and I enjoyed the work. I oversaw both his familial estate and his London residence."

"That's unusual, is it not?"

"It is, and it was a bit of a hardship for me. But his lordship would have no one but me in charge of his households."

Mr. Taggart's pride in both his work and his previous employer's faith in him was evident, as was his fondness for the old duke.

"If you don't mind me asking, why did you leave his employ?"

His face hardened, the tattoos making him look quite fierce. "The duke passed away. His family didn't see fit to retain my services."

Brynne could understand their actions, though the longer she spent in his presence, the more she liked him. A wave of pity for him filled her and she dropped her gaze, knowing he would not welcome such an emotion from her.

"When he knew he wouldn't recover, his lordship made sure I had his recommendations to take with me. However, I thought I might have better luck here than in Britain."

His tone didn't sound confident and Brynne could imagine what his experiences had been like thus far. She'd be surprised if he'd even made it past the door of any of his previous interviews.

She wavered for a moment. She generally had fairly good instincts about people and Mr. Taggart struck her as someone she could trust. He definitely had glowing references, and even her mother-in-law would be impressed with a butler who'd served an actual duke. However, one look at the man would send the elder Mrs. Forrester straight to bed for a month.

But he'd known Jake. Been his friend. Had officiated at their marriage ceremony. And he'd never find a position anywhere else.

"Well, Mr. Taggart…." The man's face had already taken on a resigned look that made Brynne's heart clench in a protective, almost motherly way. "I would be pleased to have you join my household, if you'd like to accept the position."

His relief lent a softness to his face that gave Brynne a peek at what he might have been like before the experiences that led to the tattooing of his face, and the reason behind his leaving the tribe.

"I would be happy to, Mrs. Forrester."

"Excellent. Well, we can work out all the details later. For now, why don't we have Mrs. Krause show you to your room and you can get settled."

"That would suit me very well, thank you, ma'am."

They stood and Brynne rang the little bell to call the housekeeper in. Mrs. Krause bustled in, only sparing the barest of glances for Mr. Taggart. Her entire demeanor fairly shouted haughty disdain. Brynne frowned. She hoped Mrs.

Krause wouldn't cause too many problems. Brynne knew Mr. Taggart might take some getting used to, but she was hopeful that his references would go a long way to smoothing things over with the staff. She swore servants were nearly as arrogant as their employers. Some of them were very particular about who they'd deign to serve. Brynne had felt her fair share of cold stares and begrudgingly given courtesies.

Well, Mrs. Krause would have to get used to the idea. Brynne would hate to dismiss her. A good housekeeper was harder to find than a good butler. But if Mrs. Krause couldn't accept Mr. Taggart's authority, and more importantly, Brynne's, then she'd have to be let go.

Here went nothing...

"Mrs. Krause, Mr. Taggart has kindly agreed to accept the position of butler for our household."

The older woman's nostrils flared and her eyes widened. She pinched her lips together and Brynne recognized the signs of a brewing argument so she hurried on, unwilling to get into a knock-down brawl with her housekeeper right there in the salon.

"If you could show him to his quarters and then perhaps give him the grand tour, that would be lovely. And then, please assemble the staff for me and I'll make his formal introduction."

Mrs. Krause's face turned an unhealthy shade of red and she was clenching her teeth so tightly together the muscle of her jaw audibly popped. But she didn't say anything, merely gave Brynne a cursory nod and stomped out of the room.

Mr. Taggart gathered his suitcase and turned to Brynne.

"Good luck," she said to him. It felt woefully inadequate, but there was little else she could do at the moment. Hopefully, once the woman got over her initial shock, things would smooth over.

Mr. Taggart gave her a wry smile and said, "Thank you,

ma'am," before hurrying out after the housekeeper.

Brynne slumped back into her chair and picked up the letter from her husband again. She stared at his handwriting until the words started to blur. Then she reluctantly folded it up and put it in her desk.

She didn't envy Mr. Taggart right now. But she had bigger things to worry about. She had to let her mother-in-law know who she'd just hired to be the face of her household.

Heaven help her.

Chapter Five

"Oh, madam. It's simply beautiful," Beth exclaimed, clapping her hands to her cheeks.

Brynne held the shimmering taffeta confection up to her chest so she could see it in the mirror. The deep red material brought out a becoming blush in her cheeks. It complimented her fairer skin and picked up the reddish highlights in her hair. The back of the gown erupted in a cascade of champagne colored flounces, which matched the simple, off-the-shoulder bodice. But Brynne's favorite part was a corset piece in the same dark red as her skirt that was embellished with gold embroidery.

The style was a bit unusual, but so beautiful that Brynne hadn't been able to pass it up when she'd seen it. It had been hanging in her closet for nigh on a year and while there had been many an occasion when she could have worn it, she'd always opted to remain at home instead of gadding about town. She wouldn't be wearing it to the Cabot's ball either had her mother-in-law not tricked her into going. Brynne muttered a silent curse at the woman's well-meaning meddling. Truth be told, she was rather looking forward to wearing her forgotten finery.

Beth steered her toward her dressing table first so she could have her hair done in relative comfort before donning the voluminous gown. Brynne hadn't attended many balls, despite her mother-in-law's determined efforts to get her to go to a good many of them in the year that Brynne had been in Boston. She couldn't muster the desire to hob-nob with Boston's finest when the vast majority of them viewed her as something less than pleasant that must be endured for the sake of being polite.

But Richard Oliver would be at this ball. Brynne wasn't quite sure what to think of him yet. His opinion of her appeared to be improving, which went a long way toward improving her own opinion of him. And he had agreed to let her volunteer at the clinic, which was also a mark in his favor. Those deep blue eyes and adorable dimple didn't hurt either.

Brynne's cheeks heated and she looked in the mirror at Beth's reflection over her shoulder, hoping the maid hadn't caught her tell-tale blush. But Beth was happily chattering on about the ball while she styled Brynne's hair into an elegant coif.

When she was done, Brynne turned her head from side to side, smiling as the ringlets gathered on either side of her head softly brushed her cheeks.

"Thank you, Beth. It looks wonderful."

Beth flushed with pride. "Now it's time for your gown," she said, nearly squealing with glee.

Brynne laughed. While she still felt like a cow being herded into the slaughter house, it was hard not to pick up a bit of the enthusiasm that fairly poured from her maid. Beth stuck her head into the hall and summoned Mary. They could probably manage on their own, but the help of the other maid would get the job accomplished faster, and with less potential damage to her hair.

Beth helped her step into her crinoline, and then she and Mary maneuvered her into the voluminous skirts. Beth carefully arranged them over the hoops and all three women sighed as the layers of taffeta pooled about Brynne's feet. Brynne brushed her fingertips across the material. She'd truly never worn anything so lovely in all her born days. Her heart quickened its pace a bit as a small thread of excitement flowed through her. She still didn't look forward to spending her evening with the hoity-toities, but their company was worth it for the chance to wear such a gown.

The outer girdle/corset made wearing her regular corset unnecessary, for which Brynne was truly grateful. Beth got her into the bodice, arranging the capped sleeves below the slope of her shoulders. And then the embroidered corset was fastened about her waist. Mary climbed beneath the folds of her skirts to help her slide into the black silk slippers.

Beth went to the dressing table and retrieved the jewelry Brynne would wear. Brynne hadn't owned any jewelry before arriving in Boston, other than her husband's wedding ring, her own thin gold band, and a small locket that contained a portrait of herself as a baby that Coraline had taken to wearing around the house. So these pieces had to be purchased especially to match the dress. While Brynne had never been one for frivolity, she would admit to a certain thrill at the chance to wear such beautiful gems.

Beth clasped the three-stranded pearl necklace about Brynne's neck. The large center pendant hung above the swell of her breasts, the garnet in its filigreed gold setting winking in the light of the lamps. A matching pearl and garnet comb went into her hair, and twin miniature versions of her necklace encircled each wrist. Mary held out a Spanish-style shawl made of black lace and embroidered with a delicate gold floral design. Brynne felt like a princess.

Then both of the maids stood back and enjoyed their handiwork.

"Oh, madam. You look simply lovely," Mary said.

Beth nodded in enthusiastic agreement. "You'll be the toast of the ball, no mistake about it. Dr. Oliver won't be able to take his eyes off of you."

A small squeak of protesting surprise escaped Brynne's lips. "I'm sure the good doctor will be far too busy to pay me any mind."

"No man will be too busy to notice you tonight," Beth assured her. "Some of those others you want to steer clear from, of course. They think because a woman is a widow, they can get away with taking liberties."

Beth was beginning to sound more like a protective mother hen than a ladies maid. Brynne hid her amusement, touched that the girl cared.

"That doctor," she continued, "he's a good one. An honorable man. Never been even a smattering of scandal tied to his name. And all that work he does in his clinic? He's a saint, that man. He'd be a good match," she said, with a wink.

Brynne flushed at that. "Well, I'm not looking for a good match, or any match for that matter. I'm only going to make Mrs. Forrester happy. That is all."

Beth and Mary exchanged a knowing glance that Brynne chose to ignore. She also ignored the small, inner voice that agreed with the maids. She was looking forward to seeing the doctor again. But she refused to acknowledge that, to herself or to anyone else.

Lucy entered, looking ravishing in a lavender hued work of art of ruffled tulle and lace. The women exclaimed over each other's gowns, Lucy's excitement nearly tangible in its exuberance.

The Forresters were waiting for them in the parlor and Cora came forward with an exclamation of delight.

"Oh, my dear girls, you look so lovely."

Edward, her quiet, unassuming father-in-law, nodded his shy agreement and quickly kissed her cheek. "Quite lovely," he said.

"Will it do? I know it's a bit unusual." Brynne's hand fluttered to the embroidered corset at her waist.

"It's absolutely breathtaking," Cora said. "There's a great deal to be said for standing out from the crowd."

Perhaps, but not when you were trying to fit in. Maybe the dress had been a mistake. But it was too late now. Cora had grasped her elbow and was already leading her out the door to their waiting carriage.

. . .

The moment Brynne stepped into the Cabot's grand hall, she wished she could run back out. It was, in a word, overwhelming. Between the opulence of the setting and the glittering throngs of society's elite that graced the halls, Brynne found it difficult to keep her panic at bay. What had she been thinking? She didn't belong here among the bejeweled and beribboned upper crust dancing and prattling her way through the marble-columned halls embellished with shimmering chandeliers, sparkling glass, and imported Italian marble.

But it was too late to escape. Cora led her around to various groups of chattering women, saying hello, nodding politely, and eventually stopping at a group that contained a few of Cora's particular friends. And Mrs. Morey.

Mrs. Jacobs, the one woman in the group who had always been decent to Brynne, struck up a conversation with her and Lucy. "You look so lovely tonight, Mrs. Forrester. And you as well, Miss Richardson."

"Thank you," Brynne said, Lucy echoing her. "Your gown is beautiful."

Mrs. Jacobs murmured her thanks, her cheeks blushing becomingly.

Cora gave Brynne a subtle wink and settled into a deep conversation with one of the women from her book club, content that Brynne had found a few friends to talk to.

The other women all smiled politely until the moment Cora turned her back. Then, one by one, they found an excuse to drift off. They weren't outwardly rude and did nothing blatant that shouted their disapproval. It was much more subtle. A smile that didn't quite reach the eyes, a nod of acknowledgment that was so lacking in movement it almost didn't count as a nod at all.

Brynne was surprised they bothered to keep up pretenses at all.

"Mrs. Jacobs." Mrs. Morey called to Brynne's companion. "My dear, do come and tell Mrs. Springwell about that tonic that helped George."

Mrs. Morey took Mrs. Jacobs' arm and led her away from Brynne with barely a nod in Brynne's direction. Mrs. Jacobs, bless her heart, attempted to draw Brynne along with them, but Mrs. Morey quickly waylaid her, whisking her away with a finesse that Brynne found almost admirable.

A corner of her mouth rose. *Touché, you old bat.*

Brynne turned to the other women left in their small circle, only to find them all deep in conversations with each other, a subtle turn of each back effectively shutting Brynne out.

"Excuse me," Brynne murmured, seizing the opportunity to put them all out of their misery. She made her away through the throngs of party-goers, sticking to the outer recesses of the room in search of Lucy, who had disappeared as soon as Cora's attention had been occupied. Brynne spotted her a few minutes later, happily twirling in the arms of some dashing young man. Brynne fought the slight twinge of jealousy she felt, glad that her sister was having a good time.

Brynne nodded politely whenever she bumped into someone, but with few exceptions, most didn't bother to include her, and by this time, her sensibilities were feeling too fragile for her to force her presence. Her anger grew stronger with each subtle snub. She'd never done anything to these women. Except, of course, to commit the unpardonable sin of losing her husband to a horrendous crime and then refusing to retire from society at the ripe old age of twenty-three to mourn for the rest of her days. Oh no, she insisted upon being independent and doing something meaningful with her time. How dare she?

Brynne had worked herself into a righteous lather, which was fair ready to explode, when she heard someone behind her.

"So you were able to attend after all. I was beginning to wonder."

Brynne spun about to find the good doctor gazing down at her.

"Would you do me the honor?"

He held his hand out with a slight bow. Brynne hesitated, belatedly realizing another reason she'd avoided these outings. She hated to admit to any weakness or deficiency, especially to a man who hadn't had the highest confidence in her abilities when they'd first met. But…well, she *had* grown up on a ranch outside a tiny Californian town. Learning how to dance hadn't been high on her list of priorities.

"Is something the matter?"

"Oh, well, no, it's…"

A quiet burst of tittering erupted behind her and Brynne glanced over to see Mrs. Morey and her friends smirking behind their fans. Well, that settled it. Brynne raised her chin a notch, placed her hand firmly in Dr. Oliver's, and allowed him to lead her out onto the floor.

He pulled her into his arms, wrapped his hand firmly about her waist, and spun her into the mass of swirling bodies.

Brynne stumbled and muttered an apology. Dr. Oliver smiled kindly at her. It took a few moments, but she finally figured out that if she allowed him to lead her, she could follow fairly easily.

Once she stopped concentrating so hard on where to put her feet, she began to concentrate on the rather large, warm hands that held her. She stumbled again and Dr. Oliver chuckled.

"Sorry. I didn't have much opportunity for dancing back home."

"You are doing splendidly," he assured her. "So, if you didn't spend your days dancing to your heart's content, what did you do?"

"We didn't have much time for frivolities, I'm afraid. The ranch took up all our time and what we had to spare was spent…helping any of our neighbors that needed it."

"A very worthy use of your time, indeed."

She'd almost told him exactly what sort of help she'd provided for her neighbors. Somehow, she didn't believe he'd think her bandit activities would be very worthy.

"Yes, well. We were a bit isolated there. We had to look out for each other."

"You must find life here very different."

She laughed. "A bit. Some days, I do find myself with nothing more to do than barkin' at a knot."

Richard chuckled. Brynne bit her lip and tried again. "I mean, I have more time on my hands than I'd like."

The music came to a close, but he did not release her. "Is that why you volunteered to help at the clinic?"

"Partly," she said, stepping out of his arms. "I prefer to be useful."

"Well, I'm sure we can find some task that is agreeable

to you."

Brynne nearly argued that she wasn't offering to help only as long as the task was agreeable, but the notes of the next song began and the doctor again pulled her close.

"Pardon the assumption, but I don't believe your dance card is full yet."

Brynne almost snorted but refrained. "Nor is it likely to be."

He tightened his hold on her waist and Brynne's concentration slipped again. It had been a very long time since a man had touched her, let alone held her in his arms. She'd missed it.

"This lot can be a difficult one to breach, I'll grant you that. But there are a few worth your attention."

Not many that she'd seen. Would that be an unforgivably rude thing to point out?

The doctor chuckled and Brynne ducked her head to hide her flush. Apparently, her thoughts were plainly enough written on her face that she didn't need to speak them aloud.

"I'll introduce you to a few of the more agreeable ladies."

A rush of genuine gratitude trickled throughout her. "Thank you. That is very kind of you."

The music came to an end and, true to his word, Dr. Oliver led her to a group of women that included her mother-in-law, Lucy, and Mrs. Jacobs, who were deep in conversation, and several other friendly looking faces. And Mrs. Morey. Who immediately pounced upon the poor man.

"My dear Mrs. Morey. Would you do me the honor?" Dr. Oliver bowed and extended his hand. Mrs. Morey simpered and blushed like a woman a third her age and took his hand. He led her onto the dance floor, catching Brynne's eye with a quick wink over his shoulder.

"Ah, my dear. Are you enjoying yourself?" Cora asked.

"Yes, I am," Brynne said, surprised to realize it was true.

The good doctor had made what had been a disastrous night rather pleasant.

Cora drew Brynne in to her side and introduced her to the women in the group. A few excused themselves as soon as they politely could. But a couple stayed and chatted with Brynne. Mrs. Jacobs brought over her sister-in-law and niece, who were both as friendly as she. It was refreshing to discover not every woman in the city harbored a cruel prejudice toward her, though Brynne still felt more like an exotic animal on display than a potential friend. Perhaps in time they would thaw.

And to be fair, she hadn't always been very open to meeting new people. After the first few disastrous attempts, Brynne had taken to declining any invitations that did come her way and thwarting any effort Cora made to draw her into her social circle. Brynne supposed the fault didn't entirely lay with others.

As the Forresters thanked their hostess for a delightful evening, Brynne found that she was glad that she had come. Despite the many whispers and snubs and subtle insults that had come her way during the night, she'd still found a few friendly faces with whom she'd passed a pleasant evening. And an intriguing doctor who had nearly convinced her that he might deserve a second chance before she rendered judgment.

When he sought her out before leaving in order to say goodbye and press a chaste kiss to the back of her hand, she decided perhaps he wasn't as hopeless as she'd originally deemed.

"I will see you on Monday, Mrs. Forrester. Good night," he said, bestowing a smile on her that would have charmed the knickers off a cat.

"Good night, Dr. Oliver."

Brynne wasn't sure what the next week would bring, but she was curious to find out.

Chapter Six

"All right, I believe we are ready to bind this for you," Richard said. The poor fellow had slipped while carrying his pocket knife and now sported an impressive gash on his arm. Richard had stitched him up, but wanted to keep the arm immobile for a few days to ensure the man didn't re-open the wound.

"Is it necessary to bind it to my chest, doc? I promise I won't move it. I can't stomach the notion of my arm being tied down."

"Well, it really is important to keep it steady. It will only be for a few days."

"But I won't be able to work with my arm bound so."

"Don't you worry none," Brynne said, reaching across the man to tie a large square of cloth around his neck to form a sling. "There now. This won't be at all uncomfortable. It'll lie here, all nice and cozy like."

She arranged his arm in the sling and the man gave her a grateful smile. Richard had intended to bind the arm to the man's chest much more securely, but Brynne's sling would do the trick as long as the man was careful, and he looked as if he was much happier about the arrangement.

"Thank you, ma'am. I sure appreciate it."

"No problem at all. Now you get on out of here and no more running about the house with knives in your hand. Keep that apple peeler in your pocket where it belongs."

His patient chuckled. "Yes, ma'am."

Richard smiled at her as she straightened the exam area. "You definitely have a way with the patients."

Brynne shrugged. "They simply want to be patched up so they can go about their lives. I've always found it's best to make things as easy as possible for them, especially if I want them to follow directions."

"I agree. Well, you seem to have a lot of experience working with stubborn patients."

Her lips twitched. "My sisters, mostly."

"A bit accident prone, were they?"

The smile widened a fraction. "A bit."

"I suppose there are all sorts of mishaps that can occur on a ranch."

The smile disappeared. "Yes."

Interesting. The more personal the questions he asked, the shorter her answers became. "You must miss your old home."

Brynne glanced up at him, meeting his eyes. Richard froze. She'd been working side-by-side with him for several weeks, but she so rarely looked him straight in the eyes that Richard wasn't quite sure what to do. He was afraid any sudden movements might spook her. He held absolutely still, waiting to see if she'd answer him.

She gave him a curt nod of her head and turned her attention to gathering the soiled linens from the bed.

A personal question, a no-word answer. The woman had talent.

Before he could say anything else, she murmured, "Excuse

me," and bustled out of the exam room with an armful of dirty linens. And spent the rest of the day avoiding him. Again.

No matter what he did, he couldn't seem to draw her out. She went about her work at the clinic with meticulous precision. And while she appeared to enjoy her work, as soon as she was finished, she bolted from the premises as if her skirts were on fire. When he addressed her, she answered him with short, to-the-point sentences, never deviating from the topic at hand.

He had to find a way to draw her out. He increasingly wanted to be the one to erase that haunting, sad look from her beautiful brown eyes. He wanted to see them sparkling in happiness, hear her laughter ringing through the room. She was a good woman. She deserved—

"Dr. Oliver," Mrs. Birch said, for what Richard feared was not the first time. He realized he'd been standing staring at the doorway through which Mrs. Forrester had disappeared for what must have been several minutes.

He cleared his throat, trying to hide his embarrassment at being caught mooning over some woman. He hadn't been this preoccupied with a woman since…well never.

"Dr. Oliver?"

Richard jerked his gaze from the doorway yet again. "Yes, Mrs. Birch. Pardon me, I must be a bit tired."

She patted his hand. "I was asking if we should go ahead and close up for the night. There aren't any more patients waiting to be seen and it's nearly time."

"Yes, of course. That would be—"

He caught a glimpse of Brynne near Mrs. Birch's desk. Leaning over the book where they recorded the names and addresses of all his patients. She glanced around, then quickly looked down, her finger skimming down the page. She paused for a moment, then stood and marched purposefully to the door.

"Yes, Mrs. Birch, please close up," Richard said, hurrying to the hall and grabbing his coat. He glanced out the window as he pulled on his coat, hat, and gloves. Brynne was having a word with her driver—who then nodded and drove off without her. Brynne started down the street, in the opposite direction from which she lived.

Richard waited a moment, then slipped outside.

What in heaven's name was the woman doing?

He followed her down several streets, through the bustle of the marketplace as the vendors packed up their wares for the evening, ending up in a narrow alley. Richard waited until she'd turned the corner and then ran down the length of the alley, peeking around the corner until he caught sight of her again. She was a few feet away, standing in front of the doorway of one of the rundown homes that marked the lane.

She glanced around and he ducked back, careful not to let her see him. When he peeked back around it was to see her depositing a small leather bag at the door, nudging it as close to the door frame as she could manage. She slipped a small rose from her hat onto the bag, raised her fist, and banged on the door. And then sprinted back toward the alley as quickly as possible.

Richard didn't have time to vacate his hiding place. It wouldn't have mattered anyway as Brynne had apparently been aware of his presence. She showed no sign of surprise to find him lurking in her alley. Instead, as soon as she turned the corner, she shoved him against the wall and clapped a hand over his mouth, glaring at him and bringing a finger to her lips. He nodded and she released him.

Moments later, they could hear a door being opened.

"Is anyone there?"

Brynne again motioned to him to be silent. He nodded impatiently. He wasn't sure what game she was playing at, but he was willing to follow along for a moment, if only to find out what she was up to.

"What's this?"

A few moments of silence, then a gasp. "Bess! Bess, come see!"

The door closed.

Brynne peered around the corner. Richard followed suit, ignoring another glare she aimed at him. The bag she'd left on the doorstep was gone.

"What was in—hey!"

Richard had turned to find Brynne already heading toward the other end of the alley. He jogged to catch up to her. He pulled on her arm, just enough to get her to stop. She turned to him with an impatient sigh.

"What?"

Richard's eyebrow rose a notch. "I catch you in one of the worst parts of town, leaving mysterious parcels on strangers' doorsteps, and you really have to ask, 'what'? What are you doing here? What was in that bag?"

Brynne's lips pursed together and for a moment, he didn't think she'd tell him. Finally, she blew out the breath she'd been holding. "Not here."

"What?"

"Come with me."

She didn't wait for him to agree, but turned on her heel and exited the alley. He followed her to the corner of the block where her carriage waited for her. If her driver was surprised at Richard's presence, he didn't show it, but merely opened the carriage door for them to enter. As soon as they were inside, he continued.

"Now, what is going on?"

"That was the home of Mr. Greene. The man whose arm you stitched today. He was worried about not being able to work. I simply left him something to help alleviate his worry."

Richard's eyes widened. "Such as?"

"A bit of money. It'll keep his family comfortable until he is able to provide for them again."

Richard would bet his best hat that there had been more in that bag than she implied. But that wasn't the issue of the moment.

"That is very noble of you to try to help him, but why couldn't you have given it to him at the clinic? Traveling unaccompanied in this part of town is dangerous."

Brynne snorted. "He wouldn't have taken it at the clinic, especially from me. Men are proud, Dr. Oliver, in case you were not aware. Besides, I prefer to remain anonymous."

"Well, that is all well and good, but it is still too dangerous for you to be gallivanting about on your own. Do you do this often?"

Brynne opened and closed her mouth a few times as if she were trying to come up with the right thing to say. "Not as often as I'd like."

Before he could say another word, she continued. "You don't need to worry about me, Dr. Oliver. I know how to take care of myself."

Richard was going to argue, but the carriage rumbled to a halt and the driver opened the door. Richard was surprised to find he was back at the clinic.

"Good evening, Dr. Oliver," Brynne said, clearly dismissing him.

"We'll discuss this later. In the meantime, please promise me you won't go out alone again. The next time you feel the need for this…activity, please let me know. I'd be very happy to accompany you."

Brynne looked as surprised at his words as Richard was to have said them. He hadn't meant to offer to be a party to her anonymous charity drops. He had to admit, it had been a bit thrilling to be a part of such a clandestine act. Especially one that brought so much joy to the receiver, if the tone of Mr.

Greene's voice had been any indication.

Brynne hesitated for a moment and then gave him a curt nod.

He got down from the carriage. "Good evening, Mrs. Forrester."

Brynne nodded again and the driver closed the door.

· · ·

Richard watched Brynne over the next few weeks. She never complained, never shied away from any task. And Mrs. Birch certainly set her to the worst of them, trying to get her to leave, quit. But Brynne went about them all with a smile on her face, often humming or singing to herself quietly as she went about emptying bedpans, cleaning up all manner of bodily fluids, and tending to festering sores. Despite the sometimes ghastly tasks, Brynne enjoyed her work. Even Mrs. Birch thawed when it was apparent that Brynne really was there to help and had no hidden agenda. And no designs on Dr. Oliver.

Richard frowned a bit at that. He didn't enjoy the constant attention of every unattached lady in the city. But he was accustomed enough to it that Brynne's total lack of interest in him was...noticeable. They hadn't spoken in private again since he'd caught her in her act of charity. She hadn't asked him to accompany her on any more drops, and he hoped she wasn't going on them alone. He hadn't had the opportunity to ask, as she was very careful not to be alone with him and seemed to go out of her way to avoid him.

And that simply wouldn't do.

It took him a few days to find a task that would require them to spend some time together, but once he did, he lost no time in putting his plan into action. At the first available opportunity, Richard asked for Brynne's assistance. She looked around for someone else who could help, but she was the only one available. She squared her shoulders and came toward him as if she were gearing up for battle. Curious. Was he that much of a threat?

He led her back into his office. Her gaze darted about as if she was marking her exits and he resisted the urge to laugh. Something told him she would take his amusement badly.

"What can I help you with, Dr. Oliver?"

"Please, sit down," he said, gesturing to one of the chairs before his desk. She perched on the edge of the chair, only relaxing when he settled in behind his desk.

"Would you care to join me for a bit of refreshment before we dig into details?" He gestured to a scrumptious spread of tea, delicate little sandwiches, tiny cakes, and triangle toasts with small bowls of jam. Mrs. Birch spared no effort when preparing his afternoon snack. A bit too fancy for his tastes, but for once, he was grateful for her exuberance. He wanted to make a good impression.

Brynne surveyed the items before her, her mouth already open to refuse. Richard jumped in again before she could. "Please. You've been working all morning. I'm sure you could do with a bit of food."

Brynne gave him a slight nod and accepted the cup of tea he held out to her. She selected a small cake and took a bite, her tongue darting out to catch a crumb. His eyes riveted to her mouth, to her plump lower lip that still bore a tiny smear of icing. He wondered what she'd do if he reached out and tasted it. Tasted her.

"Dr. Oliver?"

Richard blinked, bringing himself back to the task at hand. "Yes, sorry. Seems I could do with a bit of refreshment myself." He forced a chuckle and buried his nose in his teacup.

"I asked what it was you needed my assistance with."

"Oh. Yes. Well, it's a rather mundane task, I'm afraid. Some of my files were damaged when part of the roof leaked last spring and it really is vital that I transcribe them before they deteriorate to the point where they are illegible. I've been attempting to do them myself, but it's taking much longer than I'd hoped. If you'd be willing to assist me, I'd be forever in your debt."

"Couldn't Mrs. Birch? I'm sure she—"

"Mrs. Birch is always willing to lend a hand at whatever task I might have, however her penmanship is somewhat… less than desirable," he said with a small smile.

Brynne was silent and for a moment, he feared she might refuse. Thankfully, she nodded. "If I can be of some assistance to you, I will do what I can."

"Excellent. Well then, that is settled. Perhaps we could get started after I've seen my patients this afternoon?"

"I'm afraid I can't this afternoon. I must get home to my daughter."

"Ah yes, I'd heard you had a child. How old is she?"

"Coraline is almost three," Brynne answered. She fidgeted with her skirts, plucking non-existent lint from their folds.

Her daughter apparently fell into the "too personal to discuss" category. Well, he'd have to try and change that.

"Coraline. Named for her grandmother I presume?"

"Yes."

Richard waited for a moment, but as Brynne didn't seem to be forthcoming with any additional information and didn't seem interested in more refreshments, he decided to ease up on his prying. For the moment.

"Well, if she's anything like her mother, she must be a delightful child."

Brynne blushed, but he didn't torture her further. He stood and she followed suit, her face relaxing into lines of relief.

"If afternoons won't do, would you be able to come in a bit earlier tomorrow morning? We might be able to make some headway before my first patients arrive."

Brynne nodded. "I could be here by eight o'clock."

"That would be perfect."

"Well then, I will be heading home, if there is nothing else you needed to speak to me about."

There was plenty he wanted to speak to her about, but he was going to have to take his time. She was strong-minded and independent to be sure. But she also reminded him of a skittish horse he'd seen at a fair once. One wrong move and she'd bolt.

"I will see you in the morning, Mrs. Forrester."

Richard pinned his most charming smile on his lips and aimed its full strength at her. She simply stared for a moment, twitched her lips, and left the room.

His smile faded. For the first time in his life, he was at a loss at how to proceed. He'd never had to work to get a lady's attention before. Quite the opposite.

When Mrs. Birch came in, he was still staring at the door, his brow furrowed. She took one look at him and snorted, muttering something under her breath. Richard frowned at her.

"Oh, out with it if you've got something to say."

Mrs. Birch bustled around, clearing up the tea service. "That woman doesn't want anything to do with you. Or any other man, I'd wager. You've got females aplenty who'd give their best bonnet and then some for you to turn those pretty blue eyes of yours their way. Why don't you set your sights on one of them?"

Richard scowled. "Yes, and they are all alike. Every one more spoiled and prissy than the one before. I swear it's getting so I can't even tell them apart anymore. She's…different."

Mrs. Birch snorted again as she lugged the tray out of the room. "Men. Always wanting what they can't have."

Richard wondered if she had a point. Did he only want

the mysterious Mrs. Forrester because she didn't want him?

The more he contemplated it, the more he dismissed the notion. He was honest enough with himself to admit that her disinterest piqued his competitive side. But he refused to believe that was all there was to it.

Mrs. Forrester was intelligent, strong, and beautiful. And held a world of pain and secrets behind her deep brown eyes. Secrets he vowed to discover.

And his plan was already set in motion. He couldn't wait until the next morning.

Chapter Seven

The next morning came and went. No Brynne. No message.

As soon as his last patient left, Richard grabbed his coat, hailed a hackney carriage and gave the driver the Forresters' address. He was shown into the drawing room where the elder Mrs. Forrester sat with her needlework.

"Dr. Oliver, what a wonderful surprise. To what do we owe the pleasure?"

"I, ah…I actually came to call on your daughter-in-law. She had promised to help me with a project at the clinic but did not come. I wanted to make sure everything was all right."

Mrs. Forrester fixed him with a knowing glance. He had no doubt she knew exactly what he was up to. Luckily, she seemed to approve. Good. He could use an ally.

"I'm afraid my daughter-in-law no longer lives here."

Richard cursed his forgetfulness. Chasely had told him of her recently renovated home. It had completely slipped his mind.

He released a breath he didn't know he'd been holding. She wasn't at hand, but she was still nearby.

Mrs. Forrester looked back at the needlepoint in her lap, tactfully trying to hide her amusement. "She lives over on Cherry Hill Street. Usually, Coraline comes to visit me while Brynne is at the clinic, but she sent a note that the little one was feeling poorly this morning."

Richard frowned. He hoped the little girl was okay. And why hadn't her mother bothered to send *him* a note?

"Her message said that Coraline had a bit of a cold, but I'm sure Brynne would be happy to see you. Perhaps you could take a look at my granddaughter to be sure everything is all right."

"Of course, I'd be delighted to be of assistance." Richard's mood lightened considerably. Now he had the perfect excuse to drop in on her unannounced. "If you'll excuse me, I think I will head over there now."

He tipped his hat in Mrs. Forrester's direction and spun about on his heels. Before he could reach the door he realized he didn't have Brynne's address and turned back around.

"Number 412," Mrs. Forrester said with a grin.

"Thank you," Richard replied, turning before she saw his embarrassment. He hurried outside, hailed a hack, and within moments, was on his way to Brynne's new residence.

The carriage pulled up in front of an older four-story townhouse, lovely with its red brick and ivy climbing the walls. Richard grabbed the medical bag he never left the clinic without and mounted the steps leading to Brynne's door. He rang the bell and waited impatiently for it to open. When it finally did, he moved to enter, already handing his gloves and hat to the butler.

But instead of politely inviting him inside, the butler blocked his path. Richard stopped short, still holding out his hat and gloves, and froze as he got a good look at the man. The butler let him look and his eyes narrowed coldly as Richard's gaze raked over his face, pausing on his tattoos.

Richard quickly collected himself and did his best to hide his shock from the man.

"I am Doctor Richard Oliver, come to call on Mrs. Forrester."

"I'm afraid Mrs. Forrester is unable to take callers at this time," the butler said. Richard was surprised at how deep and cultured the man's voice was. Not at all the type of voice he'd expect from a man with a face full of tattoos.

Richard cleared his throat. "Yes, I'm aware that Mrs. Forrester's daughter isn't feeling very well today. Her mother-in-law asked me to stop by and take a look at her."

The butler regarded him for a moment longer and then nodded and moved aside so Richard could enter. He took Richard's hat and gloves and led the way to the fashionably decorated salon. "I'll let Mrs. Forrester know you are here, sir. If you'd be so kind as to wait a moment?"

Richard perched on the edge of a sofa. His qualms about Brynne being unprotected from outside strangers had diminished considerably. No one would get by the intimidating man guarding her door. However, the fact that that intimidating man lived in the same home as Brynne was a cause for great concern. How in the world had she come to employ such a man? Richard had to admit, he couldn't fault the butler's manners or conduct. If it were not for the facial tattoos, Richard wouldn't have given him a second thought.

Brynne opened the door to the salon and the sight of her erased all else from his mind. She looked lovely in a pale lavender gown, her chestnut tresses parted in the middle and swept into a soft bun at the nape of her neck. Richard stood and went to her without making any conscious decision to do so. He simply couldn't remain a room's length away from her

"Thank you for coming, Dr. Oliver. I do apologize for not sending a note, but it has been a busy day."

Richard took her hand and kissed the back. "Don't worry

about it at all. Your mother-in-law said that your daughter wasn't feeling well today. I thought I'd come by and give her a quick look-see."

"Oh, that's very kind of you, but I'm sure it will be a waste of your time. It's only a simple cold. But Coraline likes to have me with her when she's feeling ill."

"It would be no trouble at all. I'd be happy to take a look at her."

Brynne hesitated but in the end nodded and led him out of the salon and up a flight of stairs. They passed some open doors, bedrooms that looked neat and tidy, but unoccupied, before entering the large master suite. Brynne's cheeks flushed becomingly as she stood aside for him to enter.

"There is a nursery on the third floor, but I prefer to have Coraline close to me. She sleeps in the room adjoining mine, but she wanted to sleep with me last night and I didn't want to move her."

Warmth spread through Richard at the image of Brynne sleeping snuggled with her child all night. His own mother, while he knew she loved him, had left his main care to his nurse. He'd never been allowed to step foot into his mother's bedroom, let alone spend the night sleeping curled up with her, no matter how poorly he'd felt.

"Your daughter is a very lucky little girl to have such a mother as you."

Brynne's cheeks flushed even hotter. She didn't respond to his compliment, but instead walked over to the bed and sat down on the mattress beside a chubby-cheeked little girl with black ringlets. She looked like an angel snuggled down among the pillows and quilts.

"Coraline, this is Dr. Oliver. He's come to see how you are feeling."

Richard bent over the little girl. "Hello there."

"Hello," she answered, her voice soft and a bit hoarse, but

not at all hesitant or afraid. She was her mother's daughter for sure.

"How are we feeling today?" he asked, resting his hand against her forehead for a moment. Warm, but not distressingly so.

"My nose hurts," she said, tapping her finger on her nose a few times.

"Yes, it does sound a bit stuffy."

Coraline nodded solemnly and warmth spread through Richard's heart. What an absolute sweetheart. A young woman bustled in with a tray laden with what smelled like chicken soup. Richard nodded approvingly.

"Well, you must make sure to get plenty of rest and drink all your broth. Stay nice and warm and listen to your momma."

"Yes, sir," Coraline said quietly, giving him a shy smile. Richard smiled back at her, thoroughly charmed.

Richard looked up to find the young woman staring at him with an amused and curious expression on her face. Now that he was looking more closely, the young lady looked remarkably like Brynne, very pretty with thick dark hair framing a pert, expressive face.

"I'm Lucy," she said, not waiting for Brynne to introduce them.

He grinned, more taken with her exuberance than surprised by her forwardness.

"Very pleased to meet you, Miss Lucy. You must be Mrs. Forrester's sister."

"That would be me," Lucy said, bestowing a huge grin on him. "One of them, in any case."

"Ah yes, the other is still out west, in California, if I'm not mistaken."

Before Lucy could answer, Brynne stood. "Dr. Oliver, why don't we speak downstairs so Coraline can eat."

Coraline's little face puckered in distress, her hand on her belly. "Don't want it, Momma."

Richard frowned and bent down, smoothing Coraline's curls away from her face and feeling her forehead again in the process. A bit warmer.

"Uh oh," she whispered.

Richard jerked back, but not soon enough. The front of his suit was splattered in whatever Coraline had managed to get down earlier that day. He looked up at Brynne, who stared at him, eyes wide with surprised horror. Coraline whimpered, then hunched forward and vomited again. Avoiding being covered in the mess was a moot point, so Richard simply wrapped his arm about the little girl and held her until she'd finished.

She lay back, her pale face crumpling as she realized what she'd done. Her lip trembled. "I'm sorry."

"Don't you worry about it at all," Richard said. "Luckily, you got it all over me and not a drop on your bedding. Very smart of you," he said with a wink. He pulled the covers back up to her chin, careful not to move too much. "Perhaps it would be best to wait a bit on the soup, eh?"

Coraline nodded and gave him a tiny smile that melted his heart into a puddle of warm fuzziness.

Brynne hurried forward with a cloth and mopped up the worst of the mess while he held as still as possible. Lucy handed him a glass of water that he offered to Coraline. She took a couple sips and settled back into her pillows, curling on her side with a sigh.

Brynne kneeled down by her daughter's side and kissed her forehead. "I'll be back in a few minutes."

"All right, Momma."

Lucy settled down next to the little girl. Brynne gestured for Richard to follow her. She led him into a bedroom at the far end of the hall and rang a bell. Then she poured some water from the ewer into the basin and dampened a towel for him.

"I am so sorry, Dr. Oliver."

He stripped his soiled coat and vest, chuckling as he mopped up any spatter that had hit bare skin. "No worries at all, Mrs. Forrester. It certainly isn't the first time I've been in the line of fire."

Brynne smiled and Richard stopped his ministrations as the expression transformed her face. She was beautiful under the worst of circumstances, but when she smiled, she literally took his breath away. What he wouldn't give to make the woman laugh.

A maid hurried into the room, her eyes wide. Richard wasn't sure which sight shocked her more. The fact that her mistress was standing in a bedroom with a man, or his... disheveled appearance.

"Mary, could you ask Taggart to find some clothing for Dr. Oliver? I'm afraid there was a bit of a mishap with Coraline."

"Yes, Mrs. Forrester." The girl scurried out again, throwing a curious glance over her shoulder as she went.

Richard and Brynne stood in awkward silence. Brynne plucked at her skirts. "I am sorry I didn't send a note around, but I got busy with Coraline and..."

He waved her off. "No need to apologize, I completely understand. Your daughter, of course, must be your top priority."

"Why did you...I mean, was there something you needed?"

"Forgive me for barging in on you. There wasn't much going on at the clinic this morning, so I was hoping that we could get started on the transcriptions. When you didn't come in and didn't send word, I was a bit concerned and since I had the free time, I thought I'd drop in for a visit. Make sure that all was well."

"How did you know where I live?"

"Your mother-in-law gave me your address."

"Of course," she said with a slight blush. "Well, I'm afraid I can't come to the clinic today…"

"Oh, of course. Those can wait until you are able to return. I only wanted to assure myself that you were well."

Brynne's mouth dropped open, a bit taken aback. As well she should, he supposed. After all, they didn't know each other that well, and it certainly would have sufficed to have sent a messenger to find out why she hadn't been able to come. He didn't know what he'd been thinking, stopping by her home uninvited.

That wasn't true. He knew what he'd been thinking. His near compulsive need to spend time with the woman was getting out of hand. He couldn't get her off his mind. He'd never had a woman react to him, or not react to him, the way Brynne did. It was becoming an almost fanatical aspiration to get a rise out of her. It was distracting and beginning to affect not only his personal life but his professional one as well, which was unacceptable.

He found himself thinking of her, wondering about her, far too often. It was more than what had happened to her husband, though that would be enough to scar any woman for life. No, whatever she was hiding didn't have to do with her husband's untimely death. After all, that was common knowledge. Brynne acted like a woman with secrets. And he was determined to discover what they were. Maybe once he did, this ridiculous obsession with her would fade. She was attractive, to be sure, and he'd be lying if he said he wasn't interested in her, but he wanted to know what he was getting into before he became romantically involved with her. If she'd even have him.

That idea startled him out of his daze. He'd never considered before that a woman wouldn't want him. He'd never come across one that didn't. And if that didn't make him sound like a conceited prat, he didn't know what did.

He tried to force all such thoughts from his mind and was about to give Brynne his apologies and excuse himself as quickly as decency allowed, when Brynne spoke.

"That was very kind of you. I'm glad you came."

Richard started to respond but froze when the strange Taggart entered the room, his arms full of clothing.

"I'm sorry, ma'am, but I'm afraid the only men's clothing in the house is my own. I hope these will do."

Richard accepted the bundle from the butler. "Thank you. These will be fine, I'm sure. Anything would be preferable to what I'm currently wearing."

The butler smiled even while his nose twitched. The smell coming from Richard really was quite ghastly.

"I'll return these as soon as possible," he assured the man.

"There is no hurry, sir. If you'll leave the clothes you are wearing on the bed, I'll see that they are laundered." Taggart turned to Brynne. "Is there anything else, ma'am?"

"No, Taggart, that will be all, thank you."

He bowed slightly in Brynne's direction and turned to leave, almost bumping into Lucy on the way out.

"Excuse me, Miss Lucy."

Lucy flushed prettily as she beamed up at Taggart. "It was my fault entirely. I can be such an oaf sometimes."

Taggart ducked his head, his lips pulled into a smile that a butler had no business bestowing on his employer's young sister, and left the room. Lucy's gaze followed him until he was out of sight.

Richard wondered if he should warn Brynne about keeping an eye on her sister and Mr. Taggart, but judging by the frown on her face, Brynne was already aware of that fact.

Lucy sauntered in. "Coraline is asleep, the poor little dear. I've got her all tucked in, snug as a bug."

"Thank you, Lucy," Brynne said.

Lucy nodded and spun about, fairly skipping from the room. Brynne opened her mouth to call after her sister, but decided against it. Instead, she turned to Richard. "Well, I'll leave you to change. I really feel dreadful about…"

Richard waved her off. "Don't trouble yourself about it at all. I've never been vomited on by a more enchanting child."

A startled laugh erupted from Brynne, a funny, throaty chuckle that had Richard breaking out in a grin. He'd never heard a woman laugh quite like it before. Full-throated, from the belly, deep and pure laughter. Nothing like the simpering, "lady-like" giggles from the ladies in whose company he usually spent his time. Brynne's laugh was entirely like her; alive, invigorating, and infectious. He could listen to it all day.

"Well, then. I'll excuse myself while you…change. I'll make sure Coraline is settled. Perhaps, as you are here already…my cook has promised an especially delectable supper, trying to tempt Coraline to eat. Would you…would you care to join us?"

Richard did his best to hide his flush of pleasure at her hesitant invitation. "I'd be delighted to join you."

"I'll go tell Taggart we'll be one more then." Brynne gave him a small smile and quickly left.

A few hours with the mysterious Brynne Forrester. He stripped off his reeking shirt. It was beginning to look like a good day after all.

Chapter Eight

Brynne sent Charlie off with her note of apology with a heavy heart. Richard would surely believe she was purposely trying to get out of her agreement to help him with his documents. But while Coraline was feeling better, Lucy was not, and Cora had other engagements that morning and couldn't keep Coraline for her. She could leave her with Mrs. Krause, but Brynne didn't want to do that. Mrs. Krause was an excellent housekeeper, but she wasn't the most nurturing woman when it came to children.

So, there was no help for it. She'd had to desert Richard once again.

Not an hour had passed when there was a knock at the front door. Mrs. Krause opened it to reveal a smiling Richard, his arms laden with boxes. His man, also burdened with a large box, followed him in.

Brynne's eyes widened. "Are you moving in?"

Mrs. Krause's jaw dropped and her eyes narrowed in disapproval. Brynne's stomach sank. Would she never learn to mind her mouth? It was too late. The suggestive comment was out there.

But Richard laughed, immediately easing Brynne's worries.

"Not today, no," he said with a wink that sent a bolt of heat straight through her. "I received your note and I thought since you were unable to come to me, perhaps it would be easier if I came to you."

"Oh, I'm so sorry. What a nuisance for you."

"Not at all. On the contrary, working somewhere other than my office will do me a world of good. I spend far too much time in there."

Brynne nodded in agreement. That was certainly the truth.

"Perhaps we could work in your library?" Richard suggested, gesturing in that general direction with his overburdened arms.

"Yes, of course." Brynne chastised herself for leaving them standing in the foyer and led the way to the library.

Richard deposited his boxes on the floor near a desk and then took the box his man was carrying.

"Are these all documents?" Brynne asked, a bit dismayed at how many papers the boxes must contain.

Richard chuckled. "Not quite. These are the documents," he said, pointing to the boxes by the desk. "But that one is for Coraline."

"Coraline?"

The child in question chose that moment to come bounding into the room. She ran to Brynne, wrapping Brynne's knees in her exuberant grasp and gazing at Richard from behind her mother's skirts.

"Coraline, you remember Dr. Oliver."

Coraline nodded and gave Richard a shy smile.

Richard knelt by the large box and gestured for Coraline to come to him. "I was wondering if you could help me," he said to her as he opened the box.

Richard extracted a marionette dressed as a prince and Coraline gasped in delight. "You see, I've had this box cluttering up my attic for years and I really need the space. But I hate to say goodbye to all my childhood friends. Would you like to keep them company for me?" He pulled out another dressed as a princess, and a third dressed as a court jester.

Coraline gazed up at Richard in awe, her little face a picture of enchantment. "Yes, sir."

"Splendid. Perhaps you can get to know them while your mother and I work."

Coraline nodded eagerly. Richard spent a few minutes helping Coraline set up the small puppet theater that came with them and showing her how to jerk the strings on the puppets to make them move while Brynne watched them play and tried not to blubber.

When Richard left Coraline to her play and came back to begin work on the documents, Brynne grabbed his hand before she could stop herself. "Thank you, Dr. Oliver. That was very kind."

Richard gave her hand a gentle squeeze. "It's the least I can do, really, considering that I've invaded her home in order to steal her mother away to do my transcribing drudgery."

Brynne laughed, letting the warmth from Richard's smile seep into her. "Well, then. Let's get started."

"At your pleasure, madam," he said with a devilish grin.

Brynne couldn't help but wonder what, exactly, they were starting. Somehow, it felt as though it was much more than a simple secretarial task.

Time would tell, she supposed, as she stole another glance at the handsome doctor. Time would tell.

• • •

Brynne stared at Richard through the curtain of her eyelashes as he bent his head over the document he was transcribing. His tongue darted out and did a quick swipe of his bottom lip, a scrape of his teeth over the same area—an adorable gesture Brynne noticed he did whenever he was concentrating. The movement of his lips highlighted the dimple in his left cheek, the overall effect of which was Brynne's complete inability to concentrate on anything other than that full, delicious-looking mouth.

Which was smiling. At her.

Heat flooded Brynne's cheeks and she immediately dropped her gaze and fumbled about with the papers in front of her. They'd been working on the papers for weeks, Richard coming to her house each morning. His visits had been noticed, and naturally, tongues had been wagging like a pack of puppies with a barnyard of bones, as Cilla would say. But Richard didn't seem to mind the gossip. And neither, to her surprise, did Brynne. They weren't doing anything untoward, and she was enjoying his company. Let the Mrs. Morey's of the world spread the scuttlebutt until they were blue in the face.

The notes Brynne was transcribing were actually rather interesting. Richard's observations of certain treatments, which remedies worked best, specific cases and patients described with painstaking detail. Every word demonstrated Richard's love for, and dedication to, his profession.

Brynne absentmindedly chewed on the wooden shaft of her steel-nibbed pen as she perused the papers. The silence in the room caught her attention and she glanced up, catching Richard as he stared at her, his gaze riveted to the wood between her lips. Brynne blushed again, but Richard didn't drop his gaze. Instead, he laid aside his pen. "Let's take a break, shall we?"

Brynne nodded. It had been a slow day at the clinic, so

Richard had stayed to continue working on the transcriptions and they'd been at it several hours. "A break sounds heavenly."

Richard tugged on the bell rope that would summon a servant and when Taggart appeared he said, "Is everything ready?"

Taggart nodded. "Yes, sir. Would you like the carriage brought around now?"

"Yes, thank you. And please tell Miss Lucy."

Taggart nodded and ducked back out the door.

Brynne frowned. "Is what ready? Tell Lucy what?"

Richard held his arm out to her. "We've been working so hard on these blasted papers I decided we deserved a treat today."

He led her out of the library and Brynne's eyes widened a bit to find Lucy and Coraline waiting for them in the foyer.

Coraline ran up to her mother, bouncing up and down in her excitement. "Picnic, Momma, picnic!"

Brynne took Coraline's hand and looked up at Richard. "Well, aren't you full of surprises."

"It would be unpardonable not to take advantage of such an unseasonably beautiful day."

When they arrived at the park, a full picnic spread had already been set up for them. Richard had been right about the weather. Despite a slight nip in the air, the skies were clear with a breeze strong enough for kite flying, but not so strong as to ruin their fun. After cramming her lunch down as quickly as possible, Coraline beseeched Lucy to help her fly the kite Richard had presented her with. Richard went with them, helping to get the magnificent rainbow-colored kite airborne.

Brynne's heart skipped a beat or two as she watched Richard with her daughter. He bent over to help her with the kite string and Coraline laughed, her body nearly trembling with excitement as she watched the kite dip and soar in the sky. Lucy took over after a few moments and Richard made his way back to Brynne.

"You'll spoil her," Brynne half-heartedly warned.

Richard chuckled. "She's an angel. She deserves to be spoiled." He watched Coraline with genuine affection while she shrieked with delight and Brynne's heart skipped again.

"Thank you for today. You've made her very happy."

Richard's gaze turned to Brynne, his blue eyes washing over her with an intensity that nearly took her breath away. "And what of you? Have I made you happy?"

Lucy would probably advise her to play coy. Cilla would be all for keeping her emotions to herself until she was completely sure they couldn't be used against her. But Brynne didn't want to play any games. So she simply answered honestly. "Yes. Very happy."

He took her hand and kissed it before entwining his fingers with hers. "Then it has been my very great pleasure. One which I hope to repeat often."

Brynne took a tremulous breath, warmth flooding through her. She hoped so, too.

· · ·

Brynne sat across from Richard at her favorite café, wondering how she had managed to get herself into such a position. She was fairly sure Richard was courting her, though she wasn't sure exactly when that had happened.

He'd rarely missed a morning to work on transcribing his damaged documents. She'd realized after the first page that the task was one he could have easily set to anyone, despite his protestations to the contrary. And the task that might have taken one person a week, at most, had taken the two of them nearly a month to complete. It was obviously a ploy to spend time alone with her, something that Brynne knew she should have discouraged.

But instead of saying anything about it, she'd kept quiet. She wasn't sure why. With her own home to run, her daughter to care for, and her work at the clinic, she was no longer bored. She enjoyed Richard's company, but that in and of itself was an excellent reason to have discontinued their little sessions. He might possibly misconstrue her enjoyment of his company for romantic interest. And while she found him attractive, very attractive, every time she even began to envision herself with him, an image of her husband, with his laughing eyes and larger than life personality, would pop into her head and fill her with guilt. Yet, she'd said nothing and had continued to allow Richard to call on her.

Brynne knew many widows married again. But she couldn't seem to overcome the emotions that overwhelmed her every time she thought of Jake. They'd had such a short time together before he was ripped from her by her sadistic half-brother, his life snuffed out to further Frank's plans to take over their town.

And then there was Coraline. Brynne had a duty to her. Her life should be devoted to raising her child, teaching her everything she could about her father...not introducing a new man to take his place. No matter how wonderful that man might be.

Now their task was nearly finished. It was for the best, although Brynne's heart clenched at the notion of giving up her private time with Richard every day. She'd see him in the clinic, yes. But helping him with his patients in a roomful of people wasn't nearly as intimate as quiet moments spent poring over the files together.

He was, in many ways, Jake's opposite, in looks and personality. Richard was blond where Jake had been dark. Both men had commanding presences, but while Jake was boisterous and larger-than-life, Richard had a quiet dignity about him that commanded the respect and attention of everyone near him.

But like Jake, Richard could make her head swim with a simple look. Somehow, reacting to another man the way she'd reacted to her husband felt…wrong.

Yet here she was, lunching with him in a public place, where anyone could see them. The gossips were still atwitter about how much time they'd been spending together, closeted alone in the library for hours on end. How that information had gotten out, Brynne didn't know, but she could guess. The servants' unofficial underground network was amazing. A person couldn't do anything in Boston without the whole of the service industry passing it along. They knew *everything*. The notion that one of her staff was spreading details about her private life, however, was disturbing indeed.

There was also Coraline to consider. She was growing very attached to Richard. And he to her, if appearances could be believed. He was so sweet with her daughter that it made Brynne's heart ache to watch them together. Both with happiness and with misery. Jake should be the one playing with Coraline, reading her stories, making her giggle with his silly antics. But Jake would never be able to do any of those things.

What if Brynne was reading too much into Richard's intentions? What if he was merely being polite? Or what if Brynne couldn't get over her issues regarding Jake enough to let Richard into her life, her heart? Coraline would be crushed. Brynne didn't think her heart would ever recover from losing him either. Because, try as she might to deny it, she was falling in love with Doctor Richard Oliver. And she wasn't sure how to deal with that.

"What are you thinking about?" Richard asked, his eyes creased with concern.

"It's nothing."

He reached out and smoothed a finger over the wrinkle that had formed in her forehead. "It must be something."

Brynne sighed. No time like the present. "It's only...I've enjoyed our time together. Now that we've nearly finished..."

She couldn't go on. She'd never felt so off-balance, so insecure, in her life. She despised the feeling but couldn't seem to do anything about it.

Richard took her hand. Brynne glanced at where his hand encompassed hers, her heart skipping a beat or two as she waited for him to say something.

"I've been meaning to say something to you for weeks, but could never seem to get up the nerve."

Brynne raised an eyebrow. Richard might be kind to a fault and sweet and gentle when it came to children, but make no mistake about it—he was a man who knew what he wanted and did not take no for an answer. Brynne had once seen him reduce a vendor who had tried to swindle him to near tears. Richard Oliver was *not* a man who ever lost his nerve.

"I've enjoyed our time together as well. I would like to continue to see you, outside the clinic, after we are done with our task."

He leaned closer to her, so close his breath mingled with her own. His thumb rubbed lazy circles on Brynne's palm, shooting tingles up her arm and straight into her heart. "Would you like to keep seeing me, Brynne?"

Brynne's breath caught in her throat and her mind emptied of all thoughts but one. *Yes!*

Before she could answer, they were interrupted by a voice Brynne was beginning to think she despised above all others.

"Why Dr. Oliver, how delightful to see you here." Mrs. Morey's simpering voice wormed its way under Brynne's skin, like an itch she couldn't quite reach.

"Good afternoon, Mrs. Morey."

"You remember my daughter, of course." She thrust her

daughter forward like she was tossing a piece of meat to a starving dog.

Richard smiled, but Brynne knew him well enough now to know it wasn't genuine. It was polite, but didn't reach his eyes. "Yes, of course. It is nice to see you again, Miss Morey."

The poor girl turned beet red, her mouth gaping open like she knew she was supposed to speak but couldn't quite figure out how. Her mother frowned at her and turned her attention back to Richard.

"We stopped by the clinic earlier to offer our assistance, but your housekeeper said you were out. How fortuitous that we ran into you here."

Fortuitous my giddy aunt. Brynne had no doubt the woman had stalked any establishment within a two mile radius of the clinic hoping to arrange just such a chance meeting. And she hadn't missed the fact that the woman hadn't so much as looked in her direction the entire time she'd been standing there. For someone so well-bred, it was an incredibly bold stroke of impoliteness.

"That's very generous of you, Mrs. Morey. However, there really wouldn't be much for you to do at the clinic I'm afraid. I am fully staffed and Mrs. Forrester has been such an immense help that I don't think I'd have a single task for you. You are acquainted with Mrs. Forrester, aren't you?"

Brynne pressed her lips together to keep from smiling. Poor Mrs. Morey now had to acknowledge her. Brynne waited to see if the woman would explode.

Mrs. Morey turned a frosty smirk to Brynne. "Yes, of course. Good afternoon, Mrs. Forrester. I hope you are well."

"Very well, thank you," Brynne answered.

"Well, Mrs. Morey, Miss Morey, if you'll excuse us, we really should be going." Richard stood and offered Brynne his arm. She tucked her hand through the crook of his elbow, said goodbye as politely as she could muster, and walked away with Richard, Mrs. Morey's glare burning a hole through her back as they left.

At least one thing had been solved. With the town's biggest gossip witnessing their cozy tete-a-tete and obvious closeness, trying to decide whether or not to see Richard had become something of a moot point. The gossips would have them engaged by the end of the day. It relieved a little of the stress Brynne had been feeling. Everyone would already believe they were courting. It would be nice to actually be guilty of what the gossips accused her of, for once. And frankly, it was exhausting fighting herself over it. She wanted to see him, right or wrong.

"You never answered my question," Richard said, startling her with how closely he was attuned to her.

Brynne looked up at him and smiled, feeling suddenly shy. "Yes. I would like to keep seeing you."

"Then see me you shall, Mrs. Forrester. Brynne."

"I look forward to it. Richard."

And she meant it. The guilt was still there. She still felt like she was betraying Jake somehow. But the desire to see Richard was stronger.

For now, she was excited to see where the relationship might go.

Chapter Nine

Brynne put down her pen and stood to stretch her back. They'd been working for two hours without a break and her body was beginning to cramp from hunching over her desk. Richard had found one last file that had needed transcribing, but they'd taken their time about it. Some mornings, they had worked. Others, they'd spent walking through the park, talking and getting to know each other. They often took Coraline with them, letting her scamper on ahead as they conversed. But Richard always found a moment or two to be alone with Brynne.

It was so different from how things had gone with Jake. Jake had been impetuous, spontaneous. He'd ridden into town and swept her off her feet before she'd had two seconds to think about it. With Richard, it was no less exciting, but he took his time. Then again, had he pushed too hard, Brynne would probably have turned tail and run. She was thankful that Richard allowed her the time she needed to get used to the idea of having a new man in her life.

Brynne got a few satisfying pops out of her spine and

straightened to find Richard staring at her. Heat rushed to her cheeks. She'd grown so used to being in his company that she was starting to forget to behave properly around him. She opened her mouth to apologize and snapped it shut again, wondering what in the world she'd apologize for. Saying she was sorry for inappropriately thrusting her breasts into the air as she tried to get comfortable would most likely make matters worse.

Richard stood and grinned, then bent nearly backwards and cracked his own back. "Ah, that does feel better, doesn't it?"

Brynne felt instantly better. How did he always manage to do that? No matter how awkward or uncomfortable she might be feeling, he always knew the exact right thing to do or say to put her at ease. Richard came around to her side of the desk and half-sat on it. He took her hand and drew her nearer, so close she nearly stood between his legs as he rested against the desk.

"I've enjoyed spending these mornings with you," he said. He softly caressed her hand. Each stroke of his finger along her skin shot straight to her core, sending her normally agile mental facilities into hazy chaos.

The best response she could muster was, "Thank you."

Richard chuckled. "I hope you have enjoyed them as well?"

Buck up, woman! Brynne gathered her wits about her. She knew she should probably play coy, or feign disinterest. But frankly, she had never been one to play games. It was tiresome and dishonest. She'd always been one to speak her mind and she saw no reason to stop now, even if admitting how she was starting to feel for the doctor terrified her to the very marrow of her bones.

"I have enjoyed spending time with you. Very much." There. She'd said it and hadn't perished on the spot. Bully for her.

Richard smiled and Brynne's heart nearly jumped from her chest. "Perhaps now that we really have finished these infernal documents, we could celebrate. The annual gala for the Boston Museum is in a few weeks. I'd be honored if you'd allow me to escort you." He pulled her a fraction closer with each word, until Brynne had to crane her neck to look up at him.

Accompanying him to a society ball? A few carriage rides and walks around the park was one thing, but showing up on his arm at such a well-attended society function was tantamount to announcing their intentions before the world. What exactly were his intentions? With those blue eyes staring into hers, Brynne wasn't sure she cared.

"That sounds lovely," Brynne said, her pulse pounding so fiercely her head spun. She tilted her face towards his as he leaned down.

"You are lovely, Brynne," he said, cupping his hand around the back of her neck. "So very lovely."

Brynne hesitated for a moment. It had been such a long time since she'd been kissed. The familiar stab of guilt at the memory of the last time she'd been kissed tried to break through the happy haze enveloping her, but this time, Brynne pushed it aside. She would always love Jake, would always miss him. But he'd been gone now for nearly four years. Maybe it was time to at last let him go.

She allowed Richard to wrap her fully in his arms and rose on her toes to meet his lips.

When the library door burst open, Brynne nearly jumped out of her skin. She jerked away from Richard, her face flaming so hotly she was sure it would catch fire.

"Brynne, the most terrible thing has happened! Oh, it's altogether too horrid, it's—"

Lucy stopped mid-sentence and looked back and forth

between Brynne and Richard. Even through the tears streaming down Lucy's face Brynne could see the surprise, and approving calculation, in her sister's eyes.

"I'm sorry," Lucy said, wiping at her face. "I didn't mean to interrupt…"

"No, no, you didn't interrupt anything," Brynne said, her gaze darting to Richard who had made himself busy gathering up his documents.

"Not at all," he agreed. "In fact, we've finished up for the morning. I really should be on my way."

Brynne suppressed a rush of disappointment. Lucy was obviously very upset and now that she wasn't wrapped up in the heat of the moment, Brynne was a little embarrassed at how she'd nearly thrown herself at Richard.

He finished gathering up his things and started toward the door. He gave Lucy a polite nod and then looked at Brynne expectantly.

"I'll see you out," she said, warmth spreading through her at the loving gaze he bestowed upon her. "I'll be right back," she told Lucy.

"Take your time," Lucy said, managing to aim a teasing smirk at Brynne even through her tears.

Brynne shot Lucy a warning glance and accompanied Richard to the front door.

"I am sorry we were interrupted," he said, aiming that heart-melting smile at her again.

Brynne blushed but looked him in the eye. "As am I."

"I do hope your sister is all right."

"I'm sure she is. She's at that age where she'll pitch a fit over everything."

Richard chuckled. Then he leaned forward and brushed his lips across her cheek. Brynne sucked in her breath. She desperately wanted to pull him closer, feel the lips that caressed her cheek press against her own. Instead, she reached out with a trembling hand and opened the door.

"I will see you tomorrow, Brynne."

"Goodbye, Richard."

Brynne watched him until he had climbed into his carriage. Then she closed the door, leaning her forehead against the cool wood. Blazes, what was she getting herself into?

When she'd composed herself enough to go and deal with whatever crisis Lucy was experiencing, she turned and found Mrs. Krause standing in the hall, her sour face puckered with disapproval.

Criminy! How long had the old bat been standing there? From the look on her face, long enough to see Richard kiss her, though a peck on the cheek hardly counted in her book. Mrs. Krause's demeanor made it obvious she wouldn't agree.

Well, it was none of the housekeeper's business what Brynne did or who she did it with, so she could keep her sourpuss attitude to herself. Nothing was going to ruin the tentative happiness beginning to course through her.

"Mrs. Krause, could we have some tea and perhaps a few of those cookies Lucy likes so much sent to the library? Lucy appears to need a little cheering up."

The housekeeper gave Brynne a sharp nod and spun on her heels. She sighed. If she had any other options, she'd send the woman packing. But finding good help was hard, and for her, nearly impossible. Mrs. Krause would have to do.

For now, Brynne had bigger worries. Lucy was usually level-headed, not prone to hysterics. For her to be this upset, something truly terrible must have happened.

By the time she re-entered the library, Lucy was pacing the rug, her tears evaporated into fury.

"What's happened?"

"That, that arrogant, spineless, lying boot-licker told everyone that I...that I let him...that we...ahhh!" Lucy spun on her heels and started pacing again, her face flushed with frustrated fury.

"Lucy. Take a deep breath and calm down. You aren't making any sense and I can't help you if I don't know what's going on."

Lucy flounced onto the sofa and buried her face in her hands. Brynne gave her a moment to compose herself.

Once she calmed, she tried asking again. "Now. Let's try this again. Who exactly is an arrogant, spineless…"

"Lying bastard! Steven Bartlett, that's who. I tell you, if we were back home, I'd have him hog-tied and strung up in the barn while I introduced him to the gelding shears."

"Lucy!" Brynne tried to keep her voice stern though it was all she could do not to laugh. Lucy was normally a fairly sweet soul. But she was not someone you wanted to rile up. Brynne almost felt sorry for Mr. Bartlett, despite what he'd done to upset her sister.

"You don't know what he did!"

"And I never will if you don't calm down and tell me."

Lucy flounced back onto the sofa, her lips trembling as her rage abated somewhat. "I was at Sarah Messer's. I was so excited. I'd finally been invited to one of her super social afternoon teas." Lucy rolled her eyes. "I was so stupid. I think they only invited me to have someone to poke fun at."

Mixed in with Lucy's anger was a sort of hurt bewilderment that made Brynne's blood boil. She looked like an eager puppy who'd been kicked for being too friendly and couldn't figure out what she'd done wrong. Brynne held her tongue through sheer power of will. She didn't want to interrupt Lucy or she might never get the whole story.

"There was a whole group in attendance. Sarah, and her usual flock of followers, and several of the young men. They wanted to play a silly game. You know the one, where you hang a sheet and put a candle behind it and then disguise yourself as you walk behind it and see if the others can guess who you are. I can't help that I'm better at it than the other girls. I suspect that they play dumb to protect the boys' fragile opinions of themselves.

"I excused myself to get a bit of air. I only stepped out into the garden for a moment. But Steven followed me. I tried to go back inside but…he…he tried to kiss me."

Brynne's anger went from boiling to raging. "He did what?"

"I clouted him. It made him angry. He said I had no business putting on airs, that everyone knew what kind of women we both were, growing up wild like we did, and living with a heathen like we do." Lucy stuck her chin in the air with a satisfied grin. "So I struck him again."

"Lucy," Brynne said, forcing a note of disapproval into her voice. Truth be told, she'd rather cheer. Lying bastard indeed. Brynne would like to give the miserable little snorter a good slogging herself.

"He had it coming."

Brynne agreed but didn't voice it. "Then what happened?"

Lucy took a deep breath, her anger dissolving into hurt again. "He went back to the group. I decided I wanted to go home, so I found a maid to get my things and waited in the foyer. But before I could leave, Sarah came out. She was furious, said I was trying to steal Steven from her but that my…my whorish ways wouldn't work. He'd told everyone that I'd let him…let him…take liberties with me while we were gone. And they believed him. I'm ruined! No one will ever believe I didn't do it. I won't be accepted anywhere, no one will ever want to court me, let alone marry me. It didn't matter what I said, they believed him. And he just stood there, leaning against the doorframe, looking smug."

Lucy dissolved into tears and Brynne wrapped her in her arms, her heart breaking for her sister. She was right. That vicious bastard had ruined her, even if everything he said was a lie. And Brynne had no idea how to help her. No one would listen to her either.

"Mrs. Forrester, I'm sorry to interrupt…"

Brynne looked up to see Taggart standing in the doorway holding a tray with the tea she had ordered. Her mouth dropped open. Sweet heaven, he'd probably heard everything. By now the rumor had surely spread through half the households in Boston, so it hardly mattered.

She gathered her wits and nodded. "Please set it on the table."

He did as she directed, but instead of leaving once he'd finished, he hovered for a moment.

"Was there something else, Taggart?"

He hesitated for a second, then squared his shoulders. "Yes, ma'am. I believe I can help with the…situation Miss Lucy has found herself in."

Lucy's eyes shot to Taggart. "How?"

"I'd…rather not go into too much detail, miss. Let's just say that I can help expose the gentleman's true nature."

Brynne and Lucy exchanged a glance and before Brynne could say a word, Lucy stood. "I'd appreciate any help you could provide, Mr. Taggart."

His lips pulled into a slight smile and he nodded his head. "It will be my pleasure, Miss."

He turned to leave, but Lucy stopped him. "Mr. Taggart, I want you to know that I didn't do what he's accusing me of. I'm not the kind of girl he says I am."

"I know that, Miss Lucy," he said, his gaze lingering on her before he bowed and excused himself.

Brynne frowned. It felt like there was more going on between her butler and her sister, but she'd never seen anything inappropriate between them. She might have to keep a closer eye on the two.

• • •

Two days later, Taggart brought Brynne the morning paper, already folded open to the society pages. There was a story about the son of a prominent lawyer in town who had been caught in an extremely compromising position. He'd been found with two prostitutes in the back room of a gambling hall, so insensible with opium that he'd had to be dragged out. His name wasn't included in the article, nor was there any information about what had happened afterward.

"Steven Bartlett?"

"Yes, ma'am. It seems that his father received an anonymous note informing him of his son's preferred pastimes along with the address of where he was most likely to be found. It just so happened that a distinguished member of the press was nearby when this all occurred and was a witness to everything."

Brynne's lips twitched. Taggart hadn't been exaggerating about his ability to help.

"And what will happen to poor Mr. Bartlett now?"

"His father has decided a trip abroad might do the boy some good. His passage has already been arranged."

"You work quickly, Taggart. Nicely done."

"Mr. Bartlett made it easy, ma'am. I simply saw to it that his proclivities were exposed. I promise you that no one even remembers his lies against Miss Lucy now."

"We owe you our thanks, Mr. Taggart."

"It was my pleasure, Mrs. Forrester."

Richard came in on the heels of Mrs. Krause and sat beside Brynne. "Have you heard about this business with the Bartlett boy? Quite shocking."

Brynne's gaze shot to Taggart, who echoed her smile as he nodded to her and left the room.

Chapter Ten

The day had been relatively quiet. Only a few patients with minor ailments had come into the clinic and Brynne had spent most of the morning in Richard's office, transcribing some notes he'd made about a particularly interesting case he'd worked on. She'd become something of an unofficial secretary, a task that suited her nicely. Especially as it meant she was able to spend more time with Richard.

She'd been trying not to examine her growing feelings for him too closely. Dwelling on them brought the inevitable guilt and frankly, she was tired of feeling guilty. Jake had been dead for four years. It wasn't a betrayal of him to have feelings for another man. She only wished it didn't feel like one.

Richard filled the doorway and Brynne stopped in mid-motion, her whole body frozen as he stared at her. A slow smile stretched across his lips and Brynne's heart flipped. Richard glanced into the hallway over his shoulder and closed the door halfway behind him before he entered the room.

"Hello, Brynne."

"Hello, Richard."

She stood as he came around the desk and took the papers from her, keeping her hand in his and setting them aside without glancing at them.

How did the simple touch of his hand render her so senseless? It was both irritating and exhilarating all at once.

"How have you been getting on back here? I trust it hasn't been too wearisome."

She looked into his eyes, a smile of her own appearing to match his. "Not at all."

"Good. I'd hate to chase you away through sheer boredom."

Oh no. She could never be bored. Not with his fingers caressing her palm, reaching up to skim across the pulse jumping under the tender skin of her wrist.

He pulled her closer. Brynne's gaze flickered to the door for an instant. What if someone were to see?

Richard's other hand wrapped about her waist and she suddenly didn't care if the whole world could see them.

A cursory knock at the door heralded a very flustered Mrs. Birch. Brynne jumped and tried to pull her hand from Richard's but he kept a firm hold of it. He didn't seem startled at all by the woman's sudden appearance. He merely looked at her politely, waiting for whatever emergency had brought her running.

"Dr. Oliver, I'm sorry to disturb you, but a woman has come into the clinic with her two children. They are all ill. I believe it's scarlet fever, sir."

Richard was on the move before Brynne could take another breath. "Shut up the clinic. Has anyone had any contact with them?"

"No, sir. As soon as I saw them I put them in the small sitting room off the hall."

"Good woman. Anyone who has not had the disease must leave immediately. Tell them to burn their clothing when they get home, to be safe."

Mrs. Birch ran off to carry out Richard's orders. He turned to Brynne. "I want you to take Coraline and your sister and get out of town, immediately."

"But I can help, I've—"

"No!"

Brynne flinched, startled at his shout. Richard immediately softened and took both of her hands, drawing her close to him. "I wouldn't be able to live if anything happened to you or Coraline. Go to the country, get away from town until the sickness has passed. If this family has it, then there are others out there and there will soon be countless more. Get to safety."

He kissed her cheek, letting his lips linger against her skin. "Stay safe and well."

Richard kissed her cheek again, gave her hand a squeeze, and hurried out.

Brynne's heart clenched as she watched him go. What if she never saw him again? He didn't say whether he'd had the dreaded illness or not. And it was exactly like him to go throwing his life away to save others.

Brynne hurried out of the clinic and hailed a hack. Richard obviously didn't know her very well if he believed she'd sit back and do nothing, and she was well aware that was entirely her fault. She'd been afraid to let him get too close.

Well, Dr. Oliver was about to find out what kind of woman she was.

• • •

"But Momma, I don't want to go away."

Brynne choked back the lump in her throat as she pulled a coat around her daughter's small shoulders. "I know, chickabiddy. I don't want you to go away either. I'll miss you terribly." She pulled her in for a hug and then tilted the little girl's face up so she could look into her eyes. "But I want you to be safe and well even more. There is an illness in town, and I don't want you to catch it."

"You come too, Momma?"

For a moment, Brynne hesitated. The thought of being separated from her daughter was nearly a physical pain. But she couldn't leave Richard alone to fight the battle ahead of him, not knowing what might come of him in the process. At least if Coraline was out of the city, Brynne could rest assured that she was safe. She could not say the same for Richard. And she knew she could be of use. She had to do what she could to help.

"I can't, my darling. I will be fine," she promised her daughter. "I've already had scarlet fever, and you can only get it once. But there will be a lot of people who haven't had it before, and Momma must stay to help them."

"With Doc Liver?"

Brynne choked out a laugh at her daughter's mispronunciation of Richard's name. It had always been sweetly amusing and with the possibility of not seeing her little girl for many weeks looming, was even more so. "Yes, my love. With Doc Liver."

Coraline wrinkled her nose as she contemplated what her mother had told her. The lump in Brynne's throat grew more difficult to ignore. "I stay," she announced.

"Now young lady, your mother has told you, you must go. We'll have no more fussing from you," Mrs. Krause said. She tried to get a firm grip on Coraline, but Coraline was keen to that game. As soon as Mrs. Krause got a hold of her, Coraline went limp. The sudden shift from struggling prisoner to dead weight loosened Mrs. Krause's hold and Coraline slipped right through her fingers.

"Coraline," Brynne scolded. "That is enough."

Coraline jumped up and threw her arms about Brynne's

neck. Brynne scooped her up, holding her close. "Come on now. Brisk up. I know you are sad, but you will have a marvelous time with Aunt Lucy and your grandparents. You'll get to see the horse farm where your daddy and Uncle Leo grew up. Won't that be fun?"

"Horses?"

"Yes, there will be many horses there. Perhaps Aunt Lucy can teach you to ride. Would you like that?"

"Ride horses!" Coraline was suddenly squirming to get down, and Brynne relinquished her to Mrs. Krause.

Lucy came down the stairs, a large bag under each arm, followed closely by Taggart. Old Mr. Cotton waited by the carriage door. He'd gallantly offered to accompany Lucy and Coraline on their journey. While there was no real need for him to go, as Cora and Edward would also be there, it was no real hardship to send him along. The more people out of harm's way, the better.

The Forrester's carriage pulled up and their footman ran up the steps to help gather the bags. He stopped for a moment to give Brynne a message. "Mr. Forrester said that they'd gone on ahead to arrange passage on the train, ma'am."

"Thank you, Jimmy."

Brynne gave her daughter one more firm hug, burying her face in Coraline's curls. Perhaps she was making the wrong choice. Maybe she should go with her.

Lucy came up and held her arms out for Coraline, who gave her mother a kiss on the cheek and went to her aunt.

Brynne blinked, refusing to let the tears that threatened to fill her eyes show.

Lucy leaned in for a one-armed hug. "Ah, don't take on so. I'll take good care of her," she promised. "You don't have to worry about anything."

"She's my baby. I'm always going to worry about her."

Lucy laughed. "Well, try not to worry too much then.

She's going to have fun. It'll be like life on the ranch. Sort of."

Brynne did smile at that. Mrs. Forrester's family owned a large horse ranch in Maryland and they were taking Coraline and Lucy there. They'd promised Coraline she could ride the horses and take a trip to the beach. Brynne knew that Coraline was in good hands and would have so much fun she probably wouldn't miss home at all. But Brynne would miss her every second she was gone.

Taggart finished checking the baggage on the back of the carriage and then held out his hand and helped Coraline into the carriage as if she were a full grown lady. Her cheeks dimpled in delight. Taggart gave her a bow as she settled into the carriage and then turned to help Lucy inside. He took her hand, but instead of climbing inside the carriage right away, Lucy stood for a moment speaking quietly to him.

Brynne frowned and was about to come down the front steps when Lucy turned to wave before climbing inside to settle in with Coraline. Mr. Cotton and Mrs. Krause climbed in next and then they were off.

Brynne's heart broke a little as she watched the carriage carry her daughter farther from her. Then she squared her shoulders and went back into the house. There was work to do.

Chapter Eleven

When Richard saw Brynne walk into the clinic, her arms full of bags and parcels, his pulse quickened as it always did when he saw her. But anger and concern were quick on its heels. What was the aggravating woman doing? He had to get her out of there quickly.

He stormed toward her, but she simply thrust her bundles into his arms, gathered her skirts, and mounted the stairs. Dumbfounded, he followed along behind, holding his tongue until they were in his private quarters. Brynne went into the first room in the hallway, a guest room that he'd had rare occasion to use.

Richard dumped the parcels on the bed and rounded on her. "Are you mad, woman? What are you doing here? I told you to get Coraline to safety."

"Coraline is on her way to the Forresters' relatives in Maryland." Her voice broke a little as she spoke and she cleared her throat before she continued.

"I've had scarlet fever. And you can't take care of all the patients who will be coming in by yourself, so don't argue with me. I'm staying and I'm helping."

His worry lessened, but only marginally. He still didn't want her anywhere near his clinic. "I don't need you—"

"Sir." Mrs. Birch stood in the doorway. "Three more have come in."

Brynne nodded. "Quit your bellyachin'. You do need me." She quickly dug through one of the parcels on her bed and extracted an apron. "Mrs. Birch," she said as she put it on, "I've brought a few supplies that I had on hand. Some Epsom salts, ammonia, and all the barley we had in the house. If too many come, I feared you might not have supplies to feed them all and I know they won't be able to stomach much more than barley water."

Mrs. Birch nodded at her in approval and bustled past a flustered Richard to gather the supplies before turning to march downstairs.

Richard stood in the middle of the room, hands balled into fists by his side. Brynne looked at him with a mixture of what looked like amusement and pity. She came to him and took his hands in hers.

"My dear Richard. If you are going to court me properly there are a couple things you might want to know about me."

She suddenly had his interest. "And what would that be?" he asked, pulling her a little closer.

"First of all, I'm not one to sit idly by when there is work to be done. Secondly, and perhaps more importantly, I can be as stubborn as a mule with a knot in his tail when I want to be. It's usually best to let me have my way. Saves time." She smiled up at him and he forgot what his arguments against her staying were.

"Does that mean I have your permission to formally declare my intentions, Mrs. Forrester?" He pulled her even closer, close enough he could wrap his arms about her waist.

She hesitated for a moment before her arms tentatively

slid their way up his. "Against my better judgment, yes."

He leaned down, slowly enough that she could pull away if she wanted to, and pressed his lips against hers. They were as soft and full as he'd known they would be, and so much sweeter. She made a soft noise, something between a whimper and a sigh, and it was all he could do not to take her where she stood.

Brynne pulled away and he felt her loss immediately. She looked up at him, a soft blush staining her cheeks. But the look in her eyes was far from embarrassed. It promised much more than the small taste he'd had.

"We should go see to your patients, Richard."

He loved the sound of his name on her lips. He wanted to hear her moaning it as he—

"Richard?"

He shook his head. Heaven help him, the woman would be his undoing.

He took her arm and escorted her downstairs.

• • •

They worked non-stop, caring for the people who came into the clinic 'round the clock, catching a few moments of sleep here and there. By the end of the week, they were both on edge and ready to collapse. Still, Brynne was surprised when she came upon Richard having it out with a man she'd seen around the clinic once or twice before. The temptation to eavesdrop was great, but she had an armload of linens she needed to deliver to Mrs. Birch.

Brynne hurriedly took them to the infirmary and then went back to Richard's office. The man had gone and Richard sat behind his desk, his head in his hands

"Richard! What has happened?" She'd never seen him look so dejected, though his face was flushed with anger. A ball of anxiety formed in the pit of her stomach.

"Close the door."

Brynne hurried to comply and then sat down. "What is it?"

Richard took a deep breath. "That shipment of supplies I was waiting for…the nitre, acetate of ammonia…nitrate of silver…nearly all my stores are depleted."

The ball of anxiety turned to ice. They needed those supplies. Their patients needed them. Brynne kept quiet, not wanting to voice what she was afraid he'd say.

"It's been stolen. The entire lot. Someone intercepted the shipment before it could reach my warehouse and took every last parcel."

"Oh, Richard." Brynne let the horror of the situation sink in for a moment. Then she straightened her spine and stood up. No sense in wallowing. "What can we do about it?"

He looked at her standing before him, his brow creased in confusion, fatigue, irritation? Perhaps all three. But they had no time for any of them.

"Well?" Brynne prompted when he didn't respond.

Richard rubbed his temples. "There isn't much we can do."

"Oh, bosh. There is always something that can be done. These items aren't exactly rare. Surely there are other places you can get them."

His frown deepened. "Under normal circumstances, yes. But with the sickness spreading, everyone is running short on supplies. There is a supplier I occasionally use when there is an item I need that I can't obtain anywhere else…"

"I take it this supplier doesn't hawk their wares at the local marketplace."

Richard snorted. "Hardly. But they are very good in getting their hands on hard to get items."

"Well then. Desperate times call for desperate measures

and all that."

"These times are certainly desperate." Richard sighed and slammed his hands down on his desk, making Brynne jump. "But any other option would be preferable as it's very likely that those damn bastards were the ones to steal my shipment in the first place."

"What?" No wonder Richard looked mad enough to spit nails.

"I don't seem to have much choice," he continued. "I'll set up a meeting for tomorrow. We need those supplies."

"Well…" Brynne paused as the idea built in her head. "There might be another option."

"What do you mean?"

"I mean, I might know of another way to get our supplies back."

"And what might that be?"

Brynne hesitated again. She had no doubt that she'd be able to pull it off. She'd successfully accomplished several similar jobs to great success. However, she wasn't sure she wanted Richard to know about that part of her life. Ever. She wished Lucy were with her. It was always easier with a little help. Brynne debated telling Richard everything. She could use his assistance. But she couldn't stand to lose him if the knowledge of her past turned out to be too much.

"I can't tell you that. You'll have to trust me."

"Brynne…"

A shiver ran down her spine when he said her name. Why were names such powerful things? One little syllable on his lips and it sent a jolt straight to her heart. But she didn't have time for such things right now.

"Look, Richard, you aren't the only one who knows a few tricks to getting something that's unobtainable. But…I can't tell you more than that. Just tell me who these people are, where they can be found. Anything you know about them."

"No. Brynne, I don't want you mixed up in this. I'm touched that you want to help, but this isn't something that you can handle."

Actually, it was exactly the type of thing that Brynne handled best. She'd be lying if she said she wasn't a bit excited about the prospect of resurrecting a part of her life she'd thought done and buried. It looked like Blood Blade was going to ride again. As soon as she knew where to go.

If she could only get Richard to cooperate. Brynne studied his face. His jaw was clenched, his mouth set in stubborn lines. His eyes narrowed as if he were trying to figure out what she was up to while making sure he didn't let any important information slip. Brynne might not be the most experienced when it came to men, but she knew enough to recognize that she wasn't going to get anything out of him. But there were other ways.

"All right, Richard. I'll leave it to you." She gave him a small smile that grew wider when his eyes narrowed even further. He obviously didn't believe she was going to give up that easily.

She went to him, stood on tiptoe, and kissed his cheek. "Be careful, please."

Richard's face softened as he looked down at her. He smoothed his thumb across her cheek. "I will be." He leaned down and kissed her forehead. "I'll feel much more secure knowing you are safely out of harm's way."

A twinge of guilt wormed its way through Brynne, but she tried to ignore it. She felt the same way. She was every bit as determined to keep him safe as he was to keep her safe. The only difference was, Brynne had years of experience with this sort of thing and Richard, while he might be able to hold his own against whomever he was dealing with, still had one weakness in this scenario. He was the good guy.

Brynne was much more familiar playing the other side

of the coin. She'd have to keep her eyes and ears open so she could take care of the situation before Richard got himself mixed up in something he might not be able to control.

Brynne wrapped her arms about him as excitement flooded through her. She'd been playing the part of the well-behaved society marm for far too long.

Now it was time to have a little fun.

Chapter Twelve

Brynne knew Richard wouldn't allow her to leave the clinic while the epidemic was raging, but her new boy Charlie had become a very handy messenger who had been taking letters and messages back and forth for those quarantined in the clinic. She sent a message out to Taggart the moment Richard went back to his patients. She prayed Taggart was both loyal and able enough to do what she needed.

She didn't have to wait long. Within the hour, Charlie had returned with a parcel and a note from Taggart. Brynne tossed the boy a coin and sped up the stairs to her room. The note was simple and to the point:

I will be waiting as directed.

Brynne unwrapped the parcel. Lying inside were a pair of sturdy black trousers, a black men's shirt, a black bandana, and her long leather duster. Brynne's fingers skimmed over the soft leather of the coat. It had been a very long time since she'd worn this outfit. She hadn't been sure why she'd brought it when she'd moved east, but now she was glad she had. She couldn't do what she had planned in full skirts and corset.

Brynne stashed the clothing in her wardrobe and went back downstairs. She'd have to wait until the household had quieted for the night. There was always at least one nurse on duty, but most of those currently inhabiting the house would be tucked in their beds soon after dark.

She went impatiently about her duties for the rest of the evening, glancing at the clock in the foyer every so often. She caught Richard looking at her quizzically a few times and tried to rein in her eagerness, but it was difficult. What she was about to attempt was both foolhardy and dangerous… and completely exhilarating. And, if it worked, would both help Richard and the poor suffering souls in the clinic. She only had to wait a few more hours.

At last, it grew late and, one by one, everyone settled in for the night. Brynne went through the house, making sure all was quiet. She peeked into Richard's office. He was slumped over his desk, quietly snoring with his head pillowed on his arms. Tenderness welled up in her. She wanted to wake him and make him go up to bed, tuck him in snug and tight where he could be comfortable and get some real rest. But if she woke him, there was no guarantee he'd go back to sleep.

She closed the office door and hurried upstairs, changing as quickly as she could. She threw a dress, sans corset, petticoats, and various under-trappings, over her trousers and shirt and carried the coat in her arms. If she were seen by anyone, she didn't want it to look too strange. She secured her hair in a black hair net, wishing she could disguise it better. But the western style hat she'd worn in California would look too out of place in Boston.

Lastly, she strapped on her weapons. A gun at her hip, one in her boot, and her knife at the small of her back. It felt good to be armed again. In her old clothing, with the familiar weight of her weapons, she felt more like herself than she had in a very long time.

Sneaking quietly out the back kitchen door, Brynne hurried to the building undergoing construction down the lane, and went to the far eastern corner. The walls had been constructed, but a large hole gaped where the doorway would soon go. Brynne didn't hear anything and it was too dark to see. She was about to risk going inside when she heard a soft whinney.

"Mrs. Forrester."

Taggart had spoken softly, but Brynne still jumped. She pressed a hand to the pulse pounding in her throat and tried to calm down. If she was this jumpy before they'd even left, she'd never make it through the rest of the night.

Taggart led two horses out of the building, their hooves wrapped in cloth to help muffle the sound of their passing.

"Excellent, Taggart. Thank you."

He simply nodded and waited for her to continue. She hadn't told him much in her message. Hadn't wanted to commit too much to paper in case someone else were to see it. She'd simply asked him to bring her the parcel from the top shelf in her armoire, and to "quietly" meet her with her horse across from the clinic and hoped he'd behave accordingly. And he had. Splendidly.

She quickly filled him in on the supply situation.

His eyebrow rose slightly. "And what do you intend to do, ma'am?"

"I intend to get our supplies back, Mr. Taggart. I'm sorry to involve you, but with Lucy gone, I need someone at my back. And since you were so helpful with Lucy's situation, I hoped you might use those wonderful connections of yours to help me out again."

"What exactly do you need from me, Mrs. Forrester?"

Taggart seemed amused, not horrified, and not surprised, which Brynne took as a good sign.

"I need to know if you have any idea where I might find

the supplies that we need."

"And if I do?"

"Then, Mr. Taggart, I'll need you to watch my back while I retrieve them."

Taggart pondered for a moment, long enough that Brynne had time to worry she'd trusted the wrong man. Finally, he spoke.

"It so happens that I do know where such supplies might be kept. However, they won't be easy to get to. Would you perhaps like to arrange a deal instead? It would be far easier to purchase the items you need."

"Yes, Mr. Taggart, I'm sure it would be. And Dr. Oliver is prepared to do exactly that. However, I've always been disinclined to purchase the same item twice. I have little doubt the items in question were the same ones stolen from Dr. Oliver. I intend to see they are returned to him."

"How do you propose going about that, ma'am?"

"I…have a little experience in this area."

Taggart's eyebrows rose in disbelief and Brynne suppressed her irritation. Most men would find it difficult to believe a sweet, innocent, weak woman could be a bandit, and a successful one at that. Even Leo, her brother-in-law twice over, had had a hard time accepting it, even when he'd been faced with three gun-wielding women.

"Believe me or not, Mr. Taggart. All I really need from you is the location and your eyesight."

Taggart's smile looked terrifying in the dark, the tattooed lines on his chin making his mouth look distorted in the weak moonlight. "All right, Mrs. Forrester. I'll show you where you can find your supplies."

"Wonderful. One moment, please."

Brynne quickly removed her dress, ignoring Taggart's huff of surprise when she started unbuttoning her clothing. She rolled the dress into a ball and stowed it in a saddle bag, then shoved her arms through her coat sleeves. She hesitated about covering her face with the bandana. While she didn't want anyone to recognize her, she might pass for a man in the darkness. But with her face covered, it would be too obvious she was up to something. She left it tied about her neck. She could always yank it into place if necessary.

Taggart couldn't hide his surprise at her appearance.

Brynne sighed. "It's a very long story, Mr. Taggart."

"It's one I would very much like to hear one day, Mrs. Forrester."

Brynne laughed. "Help me get through this without getting caught and I'll tell you every sordid detail."

"That definitely makes what we are about to do worth it, ma'am."

Brynne snorted and mounted her horse. They moved out quietly, sticking to the side streets and back alleys as much as possible. There were a few poor souls out, but with the recent outbreak of scarlet fever, most people were keeping to their homes. It was too late and too cold to be out and about anyway.

Still, Brynne reveled at the feel of her old clothes on her back. The bandana still held the familiar smell of the ranch. She could almost imagine she was once again riding the trails with her sisters, on their way to a raid or on one of their trips to bring supplies to the townspeople they had helped under the guise of the outlaw.

"Blood Blade rides again," Brynne murmured.

Taggart led her to a rundown warehouse near the docks. Brynne glanced around. She couldn't see anyone, but that didn't mean there wasn't anyone there. She let her hand stray to the gun strapped to her hip, feeling some comfort in its solid weight.

Taggart pulled his horse up alongside hers and leaned in close.

"The supplies you seek are inside that warehouse, on the east end," he said, pointing toward a corner of the building. "There is a window near the back that is missing. You should be able to fit through it. It leads to a small basement area. I'm not sure where the medical supplies might be. You might need to go upstairs, but the basement is relatively secure and would be the best place to store their more valuable acquirements. I've heard they have medical supplies for sale, though I can't be positive they'll still be there."

"Do I want to know how you know all this?"

A wry smile passed his lips. "Most of it is easy enough to discover if you keep your ears open. As for the rest, I followed them."

"You what?"

"I met with them some weeks back. Afterwards, I followed them back here. The men I dealt with are certainly not the brains of the business. They had no idea they were being followed."

"Do I want to know why you were meeting with them?"

"Probably not, ma'am. I assure you, it had nothing to do with you or yours and in no way endangered your family. It was a...small personal matter."

Brynne took several deep breaths, worrying for a moment about what kind of man she'd invited into her home. His familiarity with thugs and black marketers was disturbing, to say the least. Then again, he appeared to be on her side. He might have dangerous connections, but as of yet, he'd used them to help her and her family.

And she was the last person who had the right to judge him either for his less-than-legal actions or for the company he kept. For now, at least, he'd earned her trust. "Thank you, Mr. Taggart."

"Are you intending to take all of the supplies?"

"The thought had crossed my mind," she said, trying

not to layer her words with too much sarcasm. The man was helping her after all, most likely going against his comrades. Which was something they would need to discuss if they got out of this in one piece. For now, she was grateful he was willing to double cross them to help her.

"How, exactly, are we going to do that, ma'am?"

"I hadn't quite figured that part out yet, Mr. Taggart."

Even in the darkness, she could see his eyebrows rise.

"I'll think of something."

"Very well, ma'am." His voice was thick with amusement. "If I see anyone, I will whistle."

Brynne nodded. Here went nothing. She dismounted and helped Taggart get the horses settled in an alleyway across from the warehouse.

"If I'm not back in fifteen minutes…" Brynne started.

"You aren't going to ask me to leave you, are you ma'am?"

"Hell, no. If I'm not back in fifteen, you'd better get some reinforcements and come in and save my sorry skin."

Taggart laughed. "Yes, ma'am."

If things went bad, the last thing Brynne wanted was to drag him down with her. But she had a daughter to worry about now and she had no intention of leaving Coraline orphaned if there was any help for it. She felt bad about involving Taggart, but she had to admit, having him as backup did make her feel a great deal better about skulking around in that warehouse where who-knew-what awaited her.

The warehouse appeared empty and deserted and had been for quite some time if appearances could be believed. The perfect place for a load of contraband, she supposed. Brynne followed Taggart's directions, keeping her back pressed along the side of the building as she made her way to the far eastern corner. Once there, she saw the window he said was missing. It was missing all right, but how he supposed she could squeeze through it, she had no idea. It was tiny.

There were other windows, but not many and most were several feet off the ground, higher than she could reach. There were no doors along this side of the building either. She debated scouting along the perimeter of the building for another entry point but didn't have the time to waste.

She took a deep breath and slowly blew the air out. She crouched down and looked through the window. It looked into a small basement area. The floor of the inside was sunken several feet below the level of the window. The rest of the interior of the building was so dark she couldn't make out anything for a moment. Stacks of boxes were scattered near the window and back walls. There was a faint light coming from somewhere, but it was far enough off that she should be safe enough entering through the window.

In fact, despite its ridiculous size, the window was the perfect point of entry. It was low to the ground and hidden enough that even if there were people inside, they wouldn't see her.

Brynne took off her coat, instantly missing its warmth, and then removed her gun belt. There was no way she'd fit through the window with them on. She took comfort in the fact that she still had the other gun if she needed it. She folded her coat over a few times, wrapping the gun and belt inside it, and stashed it behind a broken crate. Hopefully, it would still be there when she got back.

She nudged out the few remaining shards of glass in the frame and shimmied through the window feet first. Brynne did fine until she got to her hips. She had a terrifying moment envisioning herself being wedged halfway inside. She bet a few years ago she wouldn't have had a problem. Then again, she'd given birth since then, and hadn't been particularly active since moving to Boston. She resolved to remedy that situation as she wiggled and squirmed her way through, dropping lightly to her feet inside the warehouse.

Brynne immediately crouched down and ducked behind a stack of crates. It didn't take long for her eyes to become accustomed to the dark and she got her bearings as quickly as possible.

There were crates, piles of sacks, and miscellaneous bundles everywhere. How in the world was she going to find the supplies she needed?

Several boxes of supplies were piled up in the room, but not what she was looking for. Of course, the clinic could use everything the bastards had stashed, but without a wagon to haul it all back, there was no way she could get it all out of there. Especially not if she had to cram everything through the tiny window.

Brynne hunkered down and thought for a moment. A sound up the stairs where the light originated drew her attention and she crept closer. Two men's voices drifted to her and Brynne pressed back against the wall, her heart pounding in her throat. Muffled voices muttered about something Brynne couldn't quite catch. Something about a deal and...the doctor! They must be discussing Richard and the proposed drop for the next day.

Brynne scuttled up the stairs. The door was propped open with a box. She squeezed through the narrow opening, not wanting to open the door any farther than they already had it. She crept as close as she dared to the voices, darting behind whatever stacks of contraband that she could. She drew close to some sort of office. There were no windows looking in, but the door was ajar. Brynne tried to see inside, but ducked back behind her stack of crates when the door flew open.

Two men came out, one decidedly more scruffy than the other, his face unshaven, hair sticking out every which way. The other might have looked at home at a society function. His clothes were fashionable, if a bit threadbare. He must be the front man, the one who did the face-to-face dealings. He'd certainly make prospective buyers a little less nervous than the other man.

Sitting near the door was a small stack of boxes. The more gentlemanly man closed the door behind him. "Make sure those are ready to go tomorrow night. Only bring two of them. If the doc wants the rest of them, he'll have to double his offer."

Scruffy man laughed. "I'll have everything ready."

"Come on, hurry up. It's late." The gentleman waited impatiently by the door leading outside.

Brynne held her breath. As soon as the goons left, she could creep into the office, take the clinic's supplies back, and none would be the wiser.

"I'm coming." Scruffy said. He started toward the man by the door.

"Did you lock it?"

"Why bother? No one knows it's here and we'll be back soon anyway."

"You know the rules. Lock it up."

Scruffy huffed and pulled out a key. "Damn waste of time if you ask me."

"Well, no one was asking you. Just do it and let's get out of here."

Damn. Not that something as trivial as a locked door would stop her. But it would have made her life a lot easier had they left it open.

Scruffy locked the door and left the warehouse with the other man. Brynne waited a few moments to be sure she was alone and then hurried to the office door. She only had a few minutes until Taggart came looking for her. Though how he'd get in, she didn't know. He'd never fit through the window.

Brynne crouched down in front of the door and took out two of the pins that held her braid to her head. The lock was fairly standard, similar to dozens of others that she'd picked.

It took far longer than it once would have. She was out of practice.

Forcing herself to breathe slowly and take her time, Brynne inserted one of the hair pins into the bottom of the lock and, with the other, carefully felt inside the tumbler, easing each spring-loaded pin up until they locked in place. Then she turned the tumbler with the bottom hair pin.

Click.

She grasped the handle and turned the knob, relief flowing through her as the door opened. She wasted no time, but hurried to the stack of boxes. She popped the lid on the top box to be sure that it did indeed hold the supplies she was after. Excited tension flooded her, making her hands shake as she pulled out a small bag she'd tucked in the waistband of her trousers. She went through three of the boxes, filling her bag with as much as it would hold. Then she closed up the boxes and got out of there, closing the door behind her. Hopefully, the scoundrels wouldn't notice their contraband missing until after she was long gone.

She wasted no time in getting back to the window, not realizing until she reached it that she'd need a boost up. She dragged a large crate over and climbed up. She could barely reach the lip of the window sill, but she wouldn't be able to climb through with the bag in her arms. Brynne hated to let the bag out of her hands, but she had little choice. She hefted it up through the window and then gripped the sill to pull herself through.

But it was easier said than done. If she had one more box under her she could reach. She let go of the sill and started to climb down from her crate when she heard a noise toward the front of the warehouse. Was that the outside door? They couldn't be back already, could they? Brynne didn't want to stick around to find out.

She jumped for the sill again, this time managing to get

a good grip. She started to haul herself out, but there was nothing for her feet to push against, and her upper arm strength had grown pitifully inadequate. She tried again, this time certain she'd heard something. Desperation spurred her on and she kicked her feet, dragging herself up as far as she could. Her foot found purchase for a moment but slipped.

A large hand clamped on her arm and Brynne had to bite her tongue to keep from screaming. Taggart's face loomed in the darkness and Brynne's fear gave way to relief. He gripped both her arms and pulled her through the window, tugging hard when her hips wedged in the window frame. As soon as she was out, she scrambled to her feet.

"The supplies?"

"I have them," he assured her. "We need to go. Quickly."

Brynne didn't argue. She grabbed her coat, quickly re-strapping her gun to her hip right as a crash and shouting erupted from inside the warehouse. She and Taggart sprinted back across the street and into the alley where he'd tied their horses. They mounted and rode off into the night.

Brynne's body thrummed with excitement. She'd done it. She almost couldn't believe that she'd pulled it off. She'd so missed this feeling, this exhilaration that made every cell pulse with vitality. How she'd ever believed she could sit quietly in a parlor and preside over tea parties for the rest of her life, she had no idea. This, this feeling shooting through her veins, this is what made life worth living.

The only feeling that came close to it was when she was with Richard. Only he made her feel this vibrant, this *alive*. And with him, she didn't have to risk her life or do anything semi-illegal. A good argument for allowing their relationship to progress a bit further.

It was all she could do not to laugh out loud.

Taggart drew close to her. "Where are we taking it?"

Oh. Good question. Richard thought she was safely

tucked into bed in her room at the clinic and she needed to get back there and get him the supplies as soon as possible. But she couldn't exactly knock on the front door dressed as she was, and she didn't have time to stop and change her clothes. Dawn was approaching. Richard might already be awake, readying himself to meet his contact.

There was no help for it though. She'd try to sneak in the back, but she needed to get the supplies to the clinic before anyone saw them and before Richard left to make the drop.

"To the clinic, Mr. Taggart."

He didn't question her but steered his horse in the direction of the clinic. The closer they got, the more apprehensive Brynne became. What if Richard was already awake? What was she going to tell him?

She prayed that she'd be able to sneak in, drop the supplies on his desk, and make it back up to her room before anyone was the wiser.

Chapter Thirteen

When they reached the clinic, they rode around to the back. Brynne dismounted and Taggart handed her the bag.

"Thank you for your help tonight, Mr. Taggart."

"It was my pleasure, Mrs. Forrester."

"I believe I owe you a few explanations."

"You owe me nothing, ma'am." He paused, a small smile peeking through his staid demeanor. "I am curious, though."

Brynne laughed. "I'm sure you are. We'll have to have a chat one of these days."

"I look forward to that, ma'am. Now, you better get inside. I'll take care of your horse for you."

"Thank you."

He nodded and rode off and Brynne hurried to the back door. As she'd hoped, it was open. The sky was beginning to lighten as the sun began its ascent and the cook would already be up and about. Brynne entered as quietly as she could. She didn't see anyone, but she knew they were around somewhere. She hurried through the kitchen to the back stairs. Voices echoed to her from above and she backtracked, going out to the hallway toward Richard's office.

The door was open, the fire from the night before still crackling in the hearth. She slipped inside and placed the bag on his desk.

The door clicked shut behind her and Brynne froze, her breath catching in her throat. She knew Richard was behind her, but she was suddenly afraid to turn around. She could feel him staring at her, his gaze burning into her.

The silence stretched out until she couldn't take it anymore. She turned around and faced him.

Richard stood in the shadows, his face hardened into an expression she'd never seen on him before. It was more than angry, worse than when he'd heard that the supplies had been stolen.

He came toward her and she held her breath.

"Richard," she said.

"Do you have any idea what you've put me through?"

"I'm sorry, I really am. I didn't mean to worry you, but I can explain."

"You can explain? Explain why you are riding around town dressed like…like…" His eyes raked over her, from the trousers that hugged her legs, to the shirt that gaped open at her neck. His gaze lingered there. Brynne glanced down and gasped. Apparently her struggles to get out of the window had left their mark. Several tears and missing buttons left the fabric gaping open. Brynne gasped and pulled the shirt back together, but it didn't help much. Richard advanced on her and Brynne backed up against the desk. She'd never seen him like this. Her gentle, quiet doctor had disappeared to be replaced by this seething, smoldering mountain of a man.

He grasped her arms. "Who did this to you?"

Brynne blinked, not sure she heard him correctly. "I beg your pardon?"

"Who did this to you?" Richard's finger trailed along the

tears in her shirt. His face gentled a little when he looked at her, though she could still see the fury seething beneath the surface. "You can explain to me later why you were out in the middle of the night dressed like some gunslinger. No matter how reckless your behavior, it is no excuse for the actions of whoever did this to you. I will not rest until they are brought to justice. And heaven help them if I find them before the authorities do."

Brynne shivered at the raw fury in his voice. She almost hated to tell him the truth. But she couldn't have him roaming the streets looking for someone on whom to avenge her honor. The threat of that fury turned against her when she told him the truth made a ball of ice settle in her stomach.

"Richard, no one attacked me."

He frowned. "Then what, pray tell, happened?"

Brynne took a deep breath and dove in. *Best to get it over with quickly.*

"I was afraid for you. And angry that someone had stolen the supplies we needed so desperately and were going to make you pay all over again to get them back. So...I decided I would get them."

Richard's eyes widened in surprise, then narrowed dangerously. "You what?"

"I told you I could help. I got your supplies for you."

"You met with those people? There was no need for you to do that. Why would you spend your money to buy something I had already made a deal for? What were you thinking?"

"Richard, I didn't meet with them and I didn't buy your supplies back."

"But you said..."

"I said I got them back. I stole them."

Richard looked so surprised Brynne could have slapped him and he probably wouldn't have budged. He didn't speak, so Brynne hurried on with her explanation.

"That's why I'm dressed like this, and that is why my shirt is torn."

That snapped him out of it. "You mean they—"

"No, I tore it climbing out of a window. My hips got stuck and it was a bit of a struggle…"

Richard's gaze immediately went to her hips, his gaze growing more intense the longer he looked at her. The trousers didn't hide anything. They hugged every curve. For a moment, Brynne was afraid perhaps she had too many curves, but judging by the sudden hitch in his breathing, whatever he saw was very much to his liking.

"Richard, didn't you hear me? I got your supplies for you. Now you have what you need, and those bast…hooligans who took them won't profit from their theft at all."

His eyes widened at her near use of profanity but the truth of the situation finally sank in.

"You stole the supplies back from the thieves?"

Brynne nodded and waited for his reaction. He seemed to be hovering between surprise and disbelief. His sudden bark of laughter startled Brynne so much she jumped.

"I have been out of my mind with worry. I was about to send out a search party for you. I peeked in your room before getting ready to leave, to make sure you were all right. When I found you gone I…"

"You peeked in my room?" The thought of him coming into her room while she lay in bed sent a sudden heat shooting through her. He noticed her change in mood and looked down at her with hooded eyes.

"I'm sorry I worried you, Richard. I really am. I only meant to help."

His brow creased in confusion. "How did you manage to—"

Brynne shook her head. "That is a very long story. One I'd

rather not tell now. Can't we simply celebrate our success and leave the rest for later?"

Richard didn't seem sure what to say, but after a moment, his face relaxed. He chuckled. "You really are a mystery, Mrs. Forrester."

"I don't mean to be."

He laughed again and gazed down at her, his smoldering expression from earlier melting into something more tender, though there was still a dangerous edge to his gaze. He tucked a stray strand of her hair behind her ear, his hand lingering on her cheek. She pressed her face into his palm. Her actions during the night had restored the confidence she had lost since Jake died. She felt stronger, more empowered, than she had in years. She was done playing the ostracized outsider.

Brynne turned her face and pressed her lips against his palm.

His breath hitched and he stepped closer, his arm slipping behind her back, pressing her closer to him. She tilted her head up, her arms trailing up his to rest on his shoulders. She rose on her toes as he leaned down.

Their lips met halfway. Brynne molded herself to him, not caring if what she was doing was improper or wrong. She'd wanted this, wanted him, for far too long.

He wrapped both arms around her, lifting her off the ground and onto the desk as he tried to meld their bodies together. He bent her backwards, pressing her back against the desk, his mouth ravishing hers with a passion that betrayed every ounce of pent up frustration, anger, and fear he must have felt over the last several hours.

Footsteps echoed down the hall. Richard and Brynne froze, each of them gasping for breath as their heart rates gradually slowed.

The footsteps continued past the door.

Richard helped Brynne off the desk but pulled her close

again, cupping her face in his hands. He leaned down and gently kissed her lips.

"Brynne. Will you marry me?"

Brynne jerked back, struck dumb with surprise.

Richard looked at her. Her expression must have been as stunned as she felt because he laughed.

"Is it really such a surprise that I want you to be my wife?"

Honestly, yes, yes it was. Brynne knew it might be a possibility, of course. Men of his station didn't court a respectable woman they weren't seriously considering marrying. And they certainly didn't engage in activities such as the one they'd recently been involved in unless they were willing to marry the girl in question. Brynne had managed, for the most part, to ignore that little detail.

And even if she had known he might someday be interested enough to propose, she certainly hadn't expected it now. Not under these circumstances. Though…did that matter so much? He wanted to marry her. And she was fairly certain she wanted to marry him, no matter what she might try to tell herself in her darker moments. She definitely wanted to be with him in every way possible. She'd happily spend every waking moment with him.

But marriage wasn't something she wanted to rush into. And it wasn't something she wanted to decide right then. Too much had already happened that night. It was overwhelming. This was a decision she needed to make with a clear head.

"Brynne?"

He frowned, fine lines crinkling his eyes as he gazed at her. Brynne studied his face, her heart beating a little harder with every breath.

"Richard, I…can I…can I have a little time?"

"Of course. My apologies. I hadn't meant to blurt it out like this."

"Richard, you've done me the extreme honor of asking

me to marry you. No apologies are necessary."

He laughed and Brynne relaxed a little. He kissed her, a tender caress that made her head swim. "Take all the time you need."

Brynne kissed him back, letting her lips linger on his.

He moaned and deepened the kiss. Brynne was grateful his arms were wrapped so tightly about her or she might have made a complete fool of herself and melted into a puddle at his feet.

"On second thought," Richard said when they eventually came up for air, "try not to take too long."

Brynne laughed and her whole being flooded with happiness for the first time in longer than she cared to remember.

"I won't," she promised. In fact, she was sure she wouldn't need long at all.

Chapter Fourteen

Over the next couple weeks, Brynne didn't have much time to consider Richard's proposal. Brynne went about her duties, doing as much as she could to ease the suffering of the sick and the heartache left when their administrations failed. She did whatever she could to help Richard. Luckily, fewer and fewer cases were coming in and they had been extremely fortunate in being able to save many of those that came to them for help. The supplies Brynne had obtained went a long way toward easing the suffering of those under their care. Still, whenever they were able to carve out a few moments of time, Richard seemed to make it his mission to get Brynne to say yes.

Brynne paused, her hand still grasping the sheet of the bed she'd been stripping, her mind on Richard rather than the task at hand. She wanted to accept Richard's proposal, so very much. Especially when he touched her. A brush of his hand, a stolen kiss in the hallway, even a heated look from across the room, could make Brynne's insides turn to jelly.

But something still held her back. It was one thing

to admit she had feelings for Richard, and even that was something she struggled with. But actually marrying another man was something she hadn't ever considered she'd do. She'd no longer be Brynne Forrester. She'd be Brynne Oliver, a name that made her fairly quiver with delight. But…it felt like it would be severing the last connection she had with Jake. She'd be definitively stating to the world that she was no longer Jake's wife, but belonged to another man. And she knew it was crazy, but that felt wrong somehow.

She couldn't keep putting Richard off forever. But she did wish she could talk to someone about it. Her sisters were too far away, Cilla in California and Lucy in Maryland. But her in-laws had returned. Cora had sent a note to the clinic informing Brynne that while she and her husband had decided to come back to the city, Lucy and Coraline had remained in Maryland. They were having a good time and everyone felt it was best to keep Coraline far from Boston until the epidemic had passed.

Brynne ripped the linens from the bed she was changing with more vigor than necessary, earning her a curious stare from Mrs. Birch. Brynne turned her blushing face from the over-observant woman and marched out of the infirmary toward the kitchens to deposit the pile of dirty linens.

As she passed Richard's office, his door opened and Richard pulled her inside. She dropped the linens in her arms, stifling her squeak of surprise as he spun her around, his lips meeting hers in a quick, urgent kiss.

"Richard," she laughed, batting him away, "someone will see."

He kissed her again. "If you'd agree to marry me, I could pull you into my office whenever I wanted and no one would care a whit."

Her heart fluttered as it always did at the thought of being alone with him. She couldn't keep him waiting. It was time to make a decision.

"I'm sorry I've kept you waiting so long. Thank you for being so patient with me."

He kissed the top of her head. "I know I joke, but I do want you to be certain. I will wait as long as you need."

Brynne bowed her head and rested it against his chest for a moment. She didn't deserve him.

"I was hoping to go pay my mother-in-law a visit today. You said the worst of the epidemic was over. Now that the crisis has passed and they have returned…"

Richard paused for a moment. "Yes, it should be safe." His tone implied he understood exactly why Brynne wished to see her mother-in-law. He was a saint for understanding.

"I will have an answer for you tomorrow."

"Brynne, I meant it. You can take all the time you need. There is no rush. I want you to be sure."

She reached up on her tip-toes and kissed him, a long, lingering kiss that left them both craving more. "I will have an answer for you tomorrow," she said again.

"I look forward to the morning then."

He winked at her and went back to work, leaving her alone with her thoughts.

• • •

Brynne sat across from Cora, plucking at the handkerchief in her hands.

"So, our good doctor has proposed," Cora said. "I confess, I am not surprised."

"You aren't?" Brynne had been surprised. She still was. Why did such a wonderful man want to marry her?

Cora smiled and shook her head. "Of course not. It is as plain as the nose on your face how he feels about you. And how you feel about him."

Brynne felt the heat rush to her cheeks and focused on the twisted handkerchief in her lap. "Is it that obvious?"

"Yes. It is. So…why are you hesitating? You love him, don't you?"

Brynne took a deep breath. She'd never said it out loud. Saying it out loud would make it real. But it was time to decide once and for all. "Yes. I do love him."

"Well then," Cora said, reaching over to take her hand, "I think you've got your answer."

A lump formed in Brynne's throat. "Yes, but…"

"Ah, my dear. Jake would have wanted you to be happy. He wouldn't want you to live your life alone. He'd want Coraline to have a father to protect her. And Dr. Oliver is a good man. I couldn't have chosen a better step-father for my granddaughter if I had hand-picked him myself."

Something in Cora's tone made Brynne think her mother-in-law had done exactly that.

"Now," she said, pulling Brynne to her feet. "Go put that wonderful young man out of his misery."

Brynne laughed and hugged her mother-in-law. "Thank you, Cora. For everything."

Cora patted Brynne's cheek. "It is I who should thank you. You brought some happiness back into our lives. And being able to be near Coraline has been a blessing that we never dreamed would be possible when we lost Jake. Now, you deserve some happiness of your own."

Brynne hugged Cora. When she left, it was with a light heart and clear conscience. A new phase of her life was about to begin, one she'd never dreamed would be possible for her again. She couldn't wait to get back to Richard and start their lives together.

Brynne jumped down from the carriage and bounded up the steps of the clinic. Her whole body sang with happiness and for the first time, she didn't feel guilty about it. There would always be some sadness when she thought of Jake. But Cora had been right. He wouldn't have wanted her to live alone and miserable for the rest of her life. She wanted love, more children, a man who loved and respected her, who would be her partner, not merely her spouse. And she had no doubt that Richard was that man.

She was so excited to get inside and tell Richard that she accepted his proposal that she didn't see who was coming out of the clinic until she'd almost run smack into her. Brynne stumbled back a step and mumbled an apology.

"Good morning, Mrs. Forrester," Mrs. Morey said.

Brynne's light, happy mood threatened to deflate, but she'd be damned if she'd let the odious woman ruin what was going to be one of the happiest days of her life. "Hello, Mrs. Morey. How are you this beautiful morning?"

"Oh, I am quite well, thank you."

Brynne cocked her head. She had never heard the dreadful bitch sound so cheerful. "Well, that is good to hear. If you'll excuse me…"

"It's too bad I can't say the same for you."

"Pardon me?"

"I've just had a word with poor, dear Richard. It seems he's been laboring under a few misconceptions concerning a certain woman in his life. Being a good, Christian woman, I couldn't, in good conscience, allow him to be dragged down anymore by someone so unworthy of him."

If Brynne had had any doubt as to who Mrs. Morey meant, it would have been erased by the delighted way the woman raked her gaze over Brynne. Like a snake eyeing a particularly delectable rabbit.

"I am sure I have no idea to what you are referring."

"Oh, I'm certain you do." Mrs. Morey smirked and brushed past Brynne. "Good day, Mrs. Forrester."

A lump of dread formed in Brynne's gut. What had the

woman done? Surely, it couldn't be all that bad. Yes, there were things in Brynne's past that she needed to tell Richard, but nothing so horrendous that it would change his feelings for her, of that she had no doubt. And Brynne couldn't fathom how Mrs. Morey could have discovered anything much about her in any case. They were nearly three thousand miles away from California, and Brynne didn't think there was anyone left who would willingly spread tales about her.

She entered the clinic with a heavier tread than she had begun with, doubt sinking into her despite her best efforts to stay positive. Richard loved her. That was all that mattered. Surely he wouldn't let a bit of idle, malicious gossip change the way he felt about her.

The moment she entered the foyer, Mrs. Birch looked up from her table. "Dr. Oliver would like to see you in his office, Mrs. Forrester."

Brynne merely nodded and headed back to find Richard, her dread deepening more with every step. Why was she being summoned to his office like some misbehaving employee? She shook her head and tried to throw off her unease. Richard had asked her to marry him. He wanted her for his wife. Nothing a bitter old crone like Mrs. Morey could say would make him change his mind. For heaven's sake, Brynne had only been gone a few hours. A fine wife she'd make, suspecting her future husband's feelings were so fickle that they could be changed in a moment.

Brynne squared her shoulders and marched in to meet her soon-to-be fiancé, her head held high. She pictured Richard's happiness when she finally accepted his proposal. Maybe she'd greet him with a kiss. That would surprise him.

She knocked on the office door and opened it without waiting for him to answer. She strode into the room with a smile.

"Richard, I've made my decision. I…"

Brynne stopped mid-sentence at the look on Richard's face.

"Richard, what is it?"

For a moment, Brynne feared someone must have died. Richard's face was set in hard lines, his brow furrowed in anger...or confusion. In his hand, he clutched an old newspaper trimming. Brynne couldn't see the headline of the article, but she did recognize the illustration. It was a portrait of her brother-in-law, Leo, when he'd been elected sheriff of Bethany Ridge.

"Why didn't you tell me?" Richard asked, his voice low, quiet. Brynne would have preferred that he shouted.

"I was going to tell you everything."

"When? After we'd married and it was too late for me to change my mind?"

Brynne gasped, all the breath rushing from her lungs as if Richard had slugged her in the stomach. She almost wished he had. It would have hurt less than the anger and accusation in his voice.

"I saw no reason to share everything that happened in my past until I knew how serious you were about me. And then, when you proposed, I was afraid..."

"Afraid of what?"

"Of this! Of you reacting like this. I didn't want to jeopardize what we had together until I knew for sure that we had a future together. I would have told you everything before we married. In fact, that is what I came here to do. Until this moment, I didn't truly believe that anything I was about to tell you would change how you felt about me."

"My feelings haven't changed, Brynne. But..."

He wouldn't meet her gaze. Brynne's heart sank. But she wouldn't let that miserable woman destroy her happy future without at least trying to get him to understand.

"I love you, Richard." She didn't realize how badly she'd

wanted to say those words aloud until they passed her lips. It felt so good to at long last tell him the truth. Tell him how she felt. "I love you. And of course, I'll tell you everything. Anything you want to know. All you need to do is ask."

Richard bowed his head. Not the reaction Brynne was hoping to get from her declaration. The lump of dread hardened into ice that chilled her through and through.

What if she'd left it too late? She should have told him. At least about Leo.

"I love you, too. At least, I love the Brynne I thought I knew."

"What is that supposed to mean? I am the same person, Richard. Nothing about me has changed."

Richard waved the newspaper at her. "Everything I believed I knew about you has changed. You consorted with bandits? Perhaps even rode with them? There were rumors that your own sister was the bandit Blood Blade. Going by your recent activities with the medical supplies, I'm inclined to believe that one, though I'll admit, it's nearly impossible to fathom. What did you do, ride the trails robbing stage coaches?"

Brynne could almost laugh at the incredulity on his face. She honestly had no idea how to respond to him. She couldn't see how admitting that Cilla *was* Blood Blade, and that Brynne had indeed done her share of robbing and banditry, would ease him any. She shrugged, albeit a bit sheepishly.

Richard huffed and waved the clipping again. "And why didn't you tell me that you had married again?"

Brynne sighed. What was it about men? Jake he could handle. Jake was dead. But another husband, one who was alive? *That* was intolerable.

"I would have told you, before we went any further. But I didn't think it mattered."

"Of course it matters! Brynne, you've been married twice

now. Once to a husband who died under very mysterious and brutal circumstances, and then you almost immediately married your dead husband's brother, while you were still carrying the child of your first husband. And then your second husband divorced you to marry your own sister. How can that not matter?"

Brynne flinched. It sounded so much worse when he spelled it all out like that. "That wasn't exactly how it happened. I mean…it was but…"

"But what?"

Brynne sighed. She had no idea how to explain this where it wouldn't sound horrible. "First of all, Leo didn't divorce me, our marriage was annulled. Which means in the eyes of the law and God—"

"Yes, speaking of the law, was your *first* marriage even legal? There is supposedly no record of it. Do the Forresters know you bore their son a child out of wedlock? Do they know your marriage to their second son was annulled or do they even know about it? Did you lie to them, too?"

"I didn't lie to them or anyone else about anything, Richard, and yes, they know *everything*."

Brynne didn't know how the wicked woman had found out about her marriage to Jake not being legal. Then again, with the right amount of money and time it wouldn't have been that difficult. Brynne wasn't even sure she cared. She'd planned to tell Richard everything, and while she knew he might have a difficult time of it, his reaction was much worse than she'd imagined.

Brynne glared at him, anger beginning to replace her fear and sadness. "My marriage to Jake was binding in every way that mattered and my so-called marriage to Leo was annulled, which means by all accounts, legal and religious, it never existed. So really, there was nothing to tell you about. The marriage was never real. Never consummated. It was a sham, a protective measure to help me and my sisters. Once the… situation had been taken care of, our marriage was annulled and we both went on with our lives."

Richard shook his head. "Brynne, you must understand how…how this all looks. Annulled or not, you were married to your brother-in-law, who is now still your brother-in-law because he's married to your sister."

Yes, Brynne could see how it would look to him. She'd only come across one other divorced woman since she'd been in Boston. The poor woman had been completely shunned. No one who was anyone would receive her. Her husband and his pretty new wife fared much better. And if one past husband was enough to taint a woman's reputation, then Brynne was doubly damned.

Brynne's anger burned hotter and she tried to wrangle it in. The circumstances that had forced her into a sham marriage with her brother-in-law had been extreme and life-threatening, not only for her but for her sisters and the entire town. Richard had no right to judge her for what she'd done to keep others safe. But she tried to be fair. She could see his side, could understand the shock of what he'd learned.

"Richard, I can understand your feelings on the matter. I can, truly. But you must understand as well. I had no choice in the matter. It was literally a matter of life and death and my future wasn't the only one in jeopardy. I did what I had to do and I won't apologize for that. As soon as I could, I ended the marriage, and while we were married, absolutely nothing happened between us."

"But your first marriage…was it even a marriage? You lived with him as man and wife, but if you weren't legally married then…"

Yes, what then? Then she was a harlot who'd willingly born the bastard child of a man she'd bedded without the benefit of a pastor. Such a foul and unjust epitaph for what had been a pure and wonderful love.

A lump rose in the back of Brynne's throat. She wouldn't apologize for or be made to feel ashamed for her short life with Jake. No one had the right to sully that memory, not even Richard.

"I lived as Jake's wife for less than a month before he was murdered. Life is different out there, Richard. There isn't a pastor on every street corner waiting to legally join wayward couples in holy matrimony. We were bound before the eyes of God in the only way we were able and Jake was murdered before all the right papers could be signed."

Brynne took a deep breath and tried to keep her anger in check. Richard had a right to know what had happened in her past, yes. But no one had the right to tarnish even one memory of her past with her first love. "The only ones who have even a modicum of relevance in what occurred between Jake and I are the Forresters. And if they have no issue with it, certainly no one else has that right."

Richard sighed and leaned against his desk. "Why didn't you tell me?"

Brynne took a step closer to him. "I would have. Today. Before I accepted your proposal, I was planning on telling you everything."

Richard's gaze shot up, and for a moment he looked happy, before the shuttered look reappeared. He frowned. "I'll admit this has been hard to take in. And I might be able to understand it, but I would like to hear the whole story from you before we proceed further."

Brynne's eyes narrowed, but Richard wasn't done yet.

"The problem, you see, is that Mrs. Morey is the one who brought this little gem from your past to my attention. Which means by dinner tonight, the whole of Boston will be buzzing with it. Even if I am able to look past it, I don't know that others will."

Brynne held her breath. "What are you saying, Richard?"

"I don't know," he said, rubbing his hand over his face.

"Do you no longer love me?"

Richard's head jerked up. "Of course I still love you. This hasn't changed my feelings for you, though I wish I had heard these sordid little details from your lips instead of Mrs. Morey's."

Brynne's anger spiked. "There are no sordid details, Richard. This wasn't some shameful incident to be ashamed of. I did what I needed to do to protect those I cared about. A marriage—to a good, kind, respectable man, mind you—that was never truly a marriage was *annulled*, thereby rendered non-existent, which means there really was nothing to tell. The tittle-tattles can spin this any way they like, but nothing untoward happened, ever."

"That may be true, Brynne. But the gossip harpies are rarely concerned with the truth." He took her hands in his. "Perhaps we should take some time and wait for this to pass before we announce anything. Give the rumor mongers time to find something else to feast on."

"Richard…"

"I'm only concerned about you, Brynne, how this will affect you. And Lucy, and Coraline. The social mills haven't been too kind to you for lesser infractions than this. No sense in giving them even more meat to chew."

"Really? Your only concern is for me?" she asked, pulling her hands from his. "You seem more concerned with how everyone else will see this. I've told you the truth, Richard. So why does what happened years ago matter now unless you are concerned about your own reputation? Mine wasn't that great to begin with."

"Brynne…"

She shook her head, swallowing back her tears. She wouldn't let him see how badly he'd hurt her. How his "concern" cut through her like a blade. She squared her shoulders and faced him. "I'll make this easy for you Richard. I am sorry, but I must decline your offer of marriage."

Richard straightened. "Brynne." He reached for her, but she stepped back out of his reach.

"No, Richard. You are right. The gossip mongers will be spreading my sordid little tale from one end of Massachusetts to the other. The last thing in the world I want is for my supposed disgraceful past to reflect poorly on you."

She took another step back. "I'm sorry I didn't tell you sooner, Richard. I really am. But I truly didn't think it would matter to you. You said you loved me. It honestly didn't occur to me that something from my past, that by all accounts never happened, would make one hill of beans of a difference to you. I'm sorry to find that I was wrong."

She needed to get out of there before she lost her composure completely.

"Brynne, wait."

Brynne shook her head. "Goodbye, Richard."

She turned and fled, not caring that the tears she could no longer keep at bay were flowing down her cheeks. The bastard had made her care about him only to tear her heart to shreds at the first test. Better she find out now that he wasn't the man she thought he was. She was better off without him.

She wondered how long it would take before she believed that.

Chapter Fifteen

Brynne didn't want to give up her time at the clinic, but she wasn't sure how Richard would react if she still came in. She moped around the house for a week until at last Taggart stepped in.

"Ma'am, if I might make a suggestion?"

"Of course, Taggart."

"Go back to the clinic."

Brynne started shaking her head but stopped. Why shouldn't she? There was nothing for her to do around the house. Lucy and Coraline were still gone. Her in-laws had gone back to Maryland and a series of storms had blown in that kept them put. They'd sent a letter saying they'd return home as soon as the weather and roads permitted and assured Brynne that Coraline was having a grand time on the ranch.

That warmed Brynne's heart, thinking of her daughter playing with the animals and running about in the clean, fresh air. Perhaps Brynne should take Coraline back to California. Cilla and Leo had a child of their own now. It would be wonderful to see their children playing together, roaming the ranch and riding the horses like Brynne and her sisters had done when they were growing up.

And at least in California, she wouldn't have to deal with the ridiculous prejudice that she faced in Boston. Prejudice that was about to get much worse. She hadn't ever been the toast of the party, but at least she'd been tolerated. But since Mrs. Morey's version of Brynne's past had been spread around to all and sundry, all invitations to Brynne had ceased.

Perhaps she *should* go back to the clinic. She didn't necessarily need to see Richard. There were plenty of things she could do that would allow her to help out without bringing her into contact with him. That is, if she could get past the front door.

"What if they won't let me back?"

"At least you'll know."

Brynne pondered that for a second. He was right. No sense in sulking around when there were others with worse difficulties who could use her help.

"Taggart, would you be so kind as to bring me my cloak and tell Charlie to prepare the carriage?"

"Right away, ma'am."

When Brynne arrived at the clinic, she didn't allow herself the chance to lose her nerve. She climbed down from the carriage, marched right up the front steps, and opened the door. Mrs. Birch looked at her with surprise and, Brynne was surprised to see, pleasure.

"Welcome back, Mrs. Forrester. We're a bit busy this morning. We could use your help in the infirmary if you'd be willing to lend a hand."

"I'd be happy to, Mrs. Birch, thank you."

The woman gave her a small smile and went back to her work. Brynne was nearly speechless that the woman hadn't thrown her right out on her ear, but she certainly wasn't going to question it. She hung up her cloak and got straight to work.

. . .

Richard went about his work, his mood growing more foul by the hour. He'd been a fool to let Brynne go. Yes, she'd kept her past from him, but she hadn't deceived him, not really. She was right…what had happened wasn't nearly as bad as Mrs. Morey had made out. He'd been a fool to let the old biddy color his opinions. But he'd been so taken aback by her revelations that he hadn't known what to think. And now it was too late.

He could still see the stricken look on Brynne's face when she'd walked out of his office. He'd do anything to take it back, make it right between them. Every day that passed without seeing her was a torture he couldn't bear. *A self-inflicted torture*, he reminded himself.

He'd almost decided to march over to her house and demand that she see him when he entered the infirmary and saw her in the back making up a bed. He froze, not sure what to do. He was afraid that if he made any sudden movements he would spook her and she'd be off again.

Richard knew the moment she realized he was in the room. Her body stiffened and she darted a glance at him. Their gazes locked for a moment and he would have given anything to have her run across the room and throw herself into his arms.

But he'd destroyed any chance of that happening. Perhaps he should go to her. He took a step in her direction, but Brynne shook her head. It was a slight, almost imperceptible motion, but glaringly obvious nonetheless.

She'd come back to the clinic, not to him.

He turned around before she could see the smile that spread across his lips. She might not be willing to forgive him yet, but she had come back. Back to his clinic, his home. It was only a matter of time, he hoped, before she'd come back to him as well. And he was going to do everything in his power to make sure she did.

When his messenger boy came running in, it took a second for Richard to realize what the boy was saying.

"What? What did you say? Slow down, boy."

"Your warehouse, sir. It's burning. The fire brigade is trying to stop it, but it looks bad."

Richard stormed into the foyer and grabbed his coat from the hook. If that warehouse burned, it could ruin him. He housed much of his family's heirlooms there, treasures and antiques that he'd cleared out of the house in order to make room for his clinic. The truly valuable stuff was kept at the bank or in the vault in his bedroom, but to lose the warehouse would be a tragedy of epic proportions, as well as a sizable blow to his assets.

He hurried out the door after the lad, catching Brynne's eye as he did. He had no doubt she would be right on his heels.

Again it struck him how much he had truly missed her. How wonderful it had been to always have her at his back, no matter what the situation. He needed her, in the good times and the bad.

He was going to get her back. But first, he had to find out how much of his future had gone up in flames.

Richard watched bleakly as the fire brigade did their best to extinguish the flames tearing through his warehouse. Luckily, they had been alerted quickly and had lost no time in getting to the scene. The last thing anyone wanted was for the flames to spread to other buildings. The whole city could be ablaze in a matter of minutes. But Richard's warehouse stood near the water in a space all on its own so the dangers of the fire spreading were slim. And the fire hadn't been large to begin with.

In fact, by the time Richard and Brynne had arrived, the

flames had been mostly contained. Apparently, Richard's enemies wanted to merely warn him instead of decimating him. Which made sense, Richard thought as he looked at the note in his hand. A boy had delivered the note while the flames devoured a large chunk of his family's wealth. If the bastard thieves had reduced his fortune too much, he wouldn't be able to pay the exorbitant amount of money they wanted in exchange for the medical supplies they'd stolen.

They were giving him one last chance to make good on the deal they'd made before, the one he hadn't needed to keep because of Brynne. They had the rest of his supplies, and for double the price, he could have what remained of the shipment. Or, should he choose not to accept and make good on their original, now slightly altered deal, he could expect worse retribution.

Richard risked a glance at her. She stood staring at his building, her face set in an expression he was beginning to know well. He'd shared the note with her. No reason not to since, for better or worse, she had become involved with the knaves who'd done this. Brynne turned to meet his gaze.

"Don't worry, Richard. This time, I won't leave them anything to bargain with."

"You are not going after them again, Brynne."

"Why ever not?" she asked, seeming truly astonished.

"They are dangerous."

"Oh, bosh," she snorted and turned her attention back to the warehouse, but Richard grasped her arms and turned her back to him.

"I mean it, Brynne. I don't want you anywhere near these men."

"Richard, I appreciate your concern—"

"My concern? Damn it all, woman. I love you! No matter what has passed between us of late, nothing has changed that. I will *not* let you risk your neck over this."

Brynne's face softened and she reached up to caress his cheek. "I love you too, Richard. Which gives me even more reason to help you when I can. You need those supplies. It's my fault for leaving so much behind the first time. I'll get them for you. There is no way I'm going to allow you to pay for something that is already yours, especially after this," she said, waving a hand at his smoking warehouse.

"Brynne—"

"It isn't as dangerous as you are thinking it is. The last time it was almost too easy. I won't be in any danger."

"Last time was different," he said, pulling her away from the other spectators. "They'll be waiting for you this time."

"Despite what you think, I don't simply traipse in on a lick and a promise. I'm a little more fond of my life than that. Give me some credit, Richard. I've been doing this a long time. I know how to deal with people like this."

For a moment, he was confused. Then he remembered. Ah yes, her days riding with her sister the bandit. He still had a hard time envisioning the woman before him duded up like a notorious outlaw.

He studied the stubborn set of her chin, the determination flashing in her eyes, and knew there would be no talking her out of it. "Fine. Then I'm going with you."

"Oh no, you're not."

"I have every right to go, Brynne. It's my money, my supplies, my vendetta. And I am *not* going to let you go alone."

"I won't be alone. I have someone who will help me."

"Who?"

"That doesn't matter. It's someone I trust who has helped me before."

Richard frowned. "I'm coming, Brynne."

"You'll only be in the way. You don't know the first thing about…" Her eyes darted about the crowd and she leaned in to whisper, "This sort of thing."

"Then I guess you'll have to teach me, because you are *not* going without me."

"Excuse me, sir." A police officer approached them, looking between them with a wary look in his eye. "Is everything all right here?" He addressed that remark to Brynne with a pointed look at where Richard was grasping her arm.

"We are fine, sir, thank you. Merely a very difficult night."

"Yes, of course. Regarding that, Dr. Oliver, I have been assured that the flames have been completely extinguished and most of your property was salvaged, though there may be some smoke and water damage. The fire was set in an empty corner of the warehouse. We believe it may have been set by a squatter trying to find shelter or some such miscreant who'd perhaps been trying to warm themselves. Most of the damage was contained to a small area of the building."

Richard nodded. "I'm sure that's all it was. Thank you so much, Officer."

The policeman tipped his hat to them and went back to his men.

The moment his back was turned, Richard turned his attention back to Brynne. But she was gone.

"Damn that woman," Richard muttered. He wasn't going to let her get away with her crazy scheme. At least, not without him. He searched through the crowd for a few minutes but didn't see any sign of her. He had no idea how she'd disappeared so quickly, but he had no delusions about where she'd gone. He climbed in his carriage and told the driver to go to Brynne's house. He wasn't sure where she'd be going that night, but he was relatively sure she wouldn't be able to gad about thieving in her full skirts and bonnet. She'd need a change of clothing first. And he'd be waiting when she left her house again.

She was faster than he had assumed she'd be. He'd only

been hiding in the shadows in front of her house for about ten minutes before he spotted a dark-clothed figure leading a horse from the stables. Before she could mount, Richard stepped from his hiding place. Brynne gasped and shoved a hand against her mouth to keep from screaming.

Before Richard could say a word, he found himself flat on his back, a blade pressed to his throat.

His adventure into banditry was off to a fine start.

Chapter Sixteen

"Good evening, Taggart," Richard said.

Taggart looked down at him, one eyebrow slightly raised in surprise. "Good evening, Dr. Oliver," he said, making no move to release Richard.

Seeing Richard pinned on the ground at her feet gave Brynne a small twinge of satisfaction, but one that was quickly buried beneath a wave of fear for him. The stubborn man was going to get himself killed. He was certainly going to get in the way. But since he seemed every bit as pig-headed as she was, it looked like she was stuck with him for the moment.

"Let him up," Brynne said, her voice full of defeat.

Taggart jumped up and held a hand out to Richard. Richard accepted it, pulling himself to his feet.

"What are you doing here?" Brynne asked.

Richard didn't bother to answer. "Where are we off to?"

She scowled at him and he gave her his most angelic smile. Brynne bit the inside of her cheek to keep from smiling back. "Stay out of the way and do exactly as I tell you."

"Yes, ma'am," Richard said, his eyes gleaming in the

moonlight. If she didn't know better, she'd say he was enjoying himself.

His satisfaction faded into shock when he got a good look at her. "What are you wearing?"

Brynne sighed, seeming to remember those exact words coming from her brother-in-law Leo when he'd first seen Cilla in her men's clothing.

"You don't honestly expect me to be able to rob a warehouse in full skirts and corset, do you?"

His forehead crinkled. "I suppose not. But..." His eyes roamed over her, lingering on her trouser-encased leg that was firmly astride her horse. Richard's frown relaxed into a much more appreciative expression that had Brynne's insides quivering with delight. She did her best to stamp the feeling down. There was no time for that at the moment.

"You came in your carriage?" she asked him.

"Yes. Should I un-harness the horse?"

"No. We are trying to be as invisible as possible. The last thing we need is another horse. We don't want to take an entire posse in there."

Brynne frowned, but there was no help for it. She'd rather not take any horses at all, but they needed to be able to get out quick and carrying stolen supplies on foot wasn't going to work.

She sighed and swung up onto her horse. "Come on," she said, jerking her head at him.

Richard swung up behind her. "Try not to look so defeated. It isn't the end of the world you know."

"It might be," she muttered.

Richard chuckled and wrapped his arms about her waist, pulling her back into his chest. For a moment, Brynne forgot everything but the feel of him pressed against her, the familiar scent of him enveloping her. She'd missed him.

He nuzzled her neck, pressing a kiss to the pulse jumping

beneath the tender skin. "I've missed you," he said, echoing her thoughts.

She pressed back into him farther, tucking her head beneath his neck. It wasn't the time or place, but she couldn't think clearly with him wrapped about her. When this was all over, they were going to have a serious discussion. She hadn't forgiven him yet for his lack of faith in her, but maybe they could work through that. Later. Right now they had a job to do.

Taggart cleared his throat and Brynne straightened. Richard's arms loosened enough for her to sit forward, but he kept them about her waist.

"Let's go," she said, leading the way.

They took as many backstreets as they could, keeping to the shadows. The freezing temperature aided them. No one was out and about on such a night. Brynne was almost shivering by the time they reached the warehouse. She dismounted, pulling her coat closer about her. They tied their horses up behind the same building they had before and made sure there was no one about before they hurried across the street to the small window she'd used.

Richard followed Taggart's lead, pressing as close to the wall as they could while Brynne shimmied to the window and looked through. Pitch dark. Nothing that betrayed the presence of the thieves or anything else.

She divested herself of her coat and handed Taggart her gun. He looked at her, eyebrow raised. "We've riled them this time. Better to be prepared if necessary, and besides, I'd rather not leave it lying on the ground by the window again. I'll get it back from you when I come back out."

Taggart hesitated but nodded his agreement and Brynne turned to wiggle through the window.

Richard made a choked sound of protest as she disappeared through the window, but she ignored him and eased herself into the building, dropping to the balls of her feet behind a stack of boxes. She waited for a moment, straining her senses for any sound that might indicate she wasn't alone.

There was nothing.

Brynne crouched down and started to creep out from behind the boxes when a sound from above froze her in her steps. She looked toward the window in time to see Richard drop through it. She didn't know how he'd managed to squeeze his shoulders through and debated sending him right back out, but as he was already inside, he might as well help grab the supplies.

Taggart's angry face appeared briefly in the window. As soon as he saw that they were both accounted for, he backed off to stand guard.

Brynne glared at Richard, letting all the fear and fury raging through her show on her face. Richard flinched a bit, but didn't back off. He put his lips to her ear. "I told you, I go where you go."

Brynne shook him off with a scowl. The man was going to be the death of her.

She held her finger up to her mouth and crept around the corner of the boxes. Richard followed, close enough that he could follow right in her footsteps, but not so close that he'd hamper her movements. She led the way up the stairs toward the front of the warehouse where she'd found the supplies the first time.

There they were. Boxes of linens, equipment, and medicines that should have been in Richard's clinic. She felt Richard stiffen beside her in fury. She felt the same way, but they had no time for it now. They needed to grab the most important items and get out.

The absolute stillness of the warehouse grated at her nerves. Something was off, wrong. There was no way the thieves would leave everything out in the open with no guard.

No dogs. Not after last time. The supplies should be harder to get to, not easier. They must have expected another theft attempt. She paused again, searching the darkness for any sign of danger. But there was nothing alarming. Which in and of itself terrified her.

She and Richard crept to the box labeled *Fragile*. She looked about the space and grabbed a thin crowbar from a pile of tools near the crates.

Richard's eyes widened, a small smile creeping across his face. She pointed to her eyes and then at the inky blackness around them, reminding him he was supposed to be keeping watch.

He nodded and returned his attention to the warehouse. Faint traces of moonlight filtered in, giving them barely enough light to see by. It was helpful, but Brynne would have preferred no light at all. Hopefully, by the time they left, the clouds that had been rolling in all evening would give them more cover, though Brynne prayed the snow would hold off until they were well away. The last thing they needed was a trail of footprints in their wake.

The lid of the crate creaked as she pried the nails from the lid. The sound echoed and Brynne paused again. Nothing.

The sense of unease filled her, making her skin crawl. They needed to get out of there. *Now*.

She finished opening the crate as quickly as she could and motioned Richard over. They stared into the depths of the box.

"Which?" she whispered.

Richard quickly went over the contents, pulling out bottles and packages and handing them to Brynne. She yanked a sack from where it hung out of her back pocket and filled it with the items he handed her. The bottles clanked gently together and Brynne gritted her teeth. All this would be for naught if they shattered before they could get them home. She tried to pack the bags of herbs between the bottles to cushion them as much as possible.

After several moments, Richard turned, handing her the last of the supplies he wanted. "That should be more than enough," he whispered in her ear.

Brynne nodded and handed him the bag. He cradled it in his arms rather than let it swing free. Brynne nodded. That should help keep the items from clanking together. She replaced the lid on the box, not bothering to hammer it back down. They didn't have the time and risking the noise it would make was pointless. The thieves would know they'd been there soon enough.

Brynne and Richard made their way back to the window as quickly as they could. Once there, Richard handed her the bag and bent over, locking his hands together for her to use as a foothold. She grasped the windowsill and let Richard boost her up. She pushed the bag through and hauled herself out after it.

She looked around. Snowflakes landed on her cheeks, chilling her skin. And Taggart was gone.

Richard pulled himself out behind her, pushing through first one shoulder and then the other. Brynne grabbed an arm and helped pull him out. He stood and brushed himself off.

"Where's Taggart?" he whispered.

"I don't know, but I don't like this. He was supposed to wait for us right here." Brynne looked around, but there was no sign of her butler. "We can't wait. Let's check the alley."

Richard nodded grimly and followed her back to the alley where they'd left the horses, his eyes darting behind them often, watching as she did for any sign of being pursued. Apprehension crept through Brynne, making her spine tingle and her skin crawl. The whole heist had been way too easy. Something was definitely not right. But she wasn't going to stick around and wait for whatever it was to make itself known. They needed to get to their horses and get out of there. Fast.

They hurried across the lane and turned into the alley where their horses…were nowhere to be found.

Richard's outraged gasp echoed Brynne's own.

"That blackguard Taggart has made off with our means of escape," Richard hissed.

"We don't know that Taggart did this. Perhaps he was taken. The horses could have run off or been set loose or taken by the thieves."

Richard's gaze shot to hers, his frown deepening. "Then why didn't we see any sign of a struggle. We heard nothing."

Brynne shook her head, dread filling her to the core. "I don't—"

Click.

Brynne froze, raising her hands as she slowly turned her head to look at the man who aimed the pistol at her.

"You come along nice and quiet and no one'll get hurt." The man jerked his head to the side and stood back a little to give Brynne and Richard room to pass.

Gentlemanly of him. But Brynne wasn't in a gentle mood. She moved past him, keeping him in her side vision. When she drew level with him she squared her shoulders, then ducked and lunged, throwing her arms up to knock the man's gun arm off kilter while her shoulder rammed into his belly.

His shot went wild, the sound ringing through the quiet night. Richard shouted behind her and to his credit, didn't falter, but immediately jumped to assist her in grappling with the man. The man tried to bring his gun level again, but Brynne seized his arm and bit down hard. He howled and dropped the gun. It clattered off into a ditch and Brynne cursed under her breath. So much for shooting the bastard with his own gun. She sent up another curse at Taggart for making off with her gun.

Before she could attack again, he swung, his fist connecting with her jaw.

Brynne went sprawling, her vision flashing black and white dots. Her jaw throbbed in time with her heartbeat. Richard flew at the man with a grunt of rage, pummeling him within an inch of his life. Two more men came running around the corner and Brynne shouted a warning.

Richard jumped off the man he was on, since he didn't seem likely to go anywhere, and rushed to Brynne. He pulled her to her feet and they both stood ready when the other men reached them. Brynne reached behind her and grabbed the knife she kept in a sheath at the small of her back. The men rushing them slowed when they saw the weapon, still advancing, but more warily.

Richard's eyes widened, but again, his reaction surprised her. "Got another one of those?"

Brynne grinned. "As a matter of fact, I do." She reached down and pulled the knife she always kept in her boot. "Be careful with that," she said, handing it to him.

Richard snorted. "You're just full of surprises, aren't you?"

"You have no idea. Watch out!"

The men had gotten tired of circling them and came at them in a rush. Brynne tried to ignore what was going on with Richard and keep her attention on her own opponent, but every shout and grunt made it a chore to keep her wits on her own problems. Well-bred Richard wasn't as used to hand-to-hand combat as Brynne, and she feared how he was faring.

Although, if his man was as inept as the one fighting her, Richard was probably doing fine. It never ceased to amaze her how many men would underestimate a woman solely based on her gender. It didn't matter that she stood there holding a knife as long as her forearm. She was female and therefore, in most men's minds, not a threat. She was only too happy to show the imbecile in front of her how wrong he was.

The man circled her with a leering grin. "Come on, lovey. Put that toad sticker down before you hurt somebody. Come on, be a nice girl and maybe old Tommy'll take it easy on you."

"I wasn't raised to be a nice girl," Brynne said.

Old Tommy lunged at her but Brynne saw the move coming and easily dodged him. She slashed his arm, not bothering to hide her satisfaction when he howled in pain.

"You'll pay for that, you little bitch."

"Promises, promises."

He came at her again with renewed effort, trying his hardest to land some blows while staying out of range of her knife. She managed to cut him once more, but on her third attempt, he blocked her, getting hold of her wrist and twisting around until she cried out in pain and was forced to drop the knife.

He laughed, his foul breath gagging her as he dragged her close. "Now we'll have a bit o' fun, shall we?"

The noises from Richard's side of the alley were growing more intense and desperate. She needed to end this little tete-a-tete and get Richard out of there before more of the goons showed up and they were seriously out numbered.

"I'm afraid I'll have to decline your kind invitation," Brynne said. "I've had enough fun for one night."

She dropped to the ground, ignoring the painful wrench in her shoulder and rolled. The sudden change in position jerked her arm from the man's grip. Brynne rolled onto her back, drew her feet up against her chest, and kicked out with all her strength, ramming her feet into the man's knee caps.

Good old Tommy dropped, bellowing loud enough to wake the dead. Brynne retrieved her knife and ran toward Richard and his man.

"Richard," she gasped, his name escaping her lips before she could stop it.

Richard pulled his attention from his opponent for a split

second. But that was all the man needed. He lunged, the blade in his hand flashing silver in the moonlight. Brynne called out a warning and Richard jumped to the side.

But he wasn't quite fast enough. The blade slashed across his thigh, opening a streak of red that splattered against the brick wall next to him. Richard shouted and went down.

Brynne swallowed the scream that was trying to claw its way out of her throat and got a firm grip on her knife. She rushed toward them, thankful the goon had all his attention on Richard. When she reached them, she gripped the heavy handle of her blade and slammed it into the man's skull. He dropped like a sack of flour and lay unmoving on the ground at Richard's feet.

The man Brynne had fought was still howling in the corner of the alley, trying to drag himself to his feet. Brynne was pretty sure she'd dislocated at least one of his knees, so he wasn't going anywhere in a hurry. But the racket he was making was sure to bring someone running.

Brynne stooped and wrapped an arm around Richard's waist. "Come on," she said, grunting as she helped him stand. "We've got to get out of here."

Richard nodded and got himself upright. Brynne turned to steer him out of the alley, but Richard pulled against her. "Wait."

He broke from her grasp, ignoring her hiss of impatience. He hopped over to the sack lying against the wall and gathered it up.

"It would be a shame to go through all this for naught," he said with a wry grin.

Brynne's lips twitched. "Good point. Now we must hurry!"

"One more thing." Richard limped toward the man Brynne had felled and leaned down. "If I were less than a gentleman, I'd do much worse to you than this. But I do not have the time to give you what you really deserve."

"Go to hell."

Richard slammed his fist into the man's face. "You first," he muttered.

Chapter Seventeen

Richard's hand throbbed and his stomach clenched at the sight of the man crumpling under his fist. He'd never struck a man so forcefully in his life. But he'd do worse than that if it kept Brynne from danger.

Brynne cocked an eyebrow at him.

"We couldn't very well have him crawling off to find his mates or sounding the alarm."

Brynne nodded in agreement, but she looked a bit unsettled, as if she wasn't sure what to make of the more ruthless side of him. Of course, she'd never seen anything but the kind, gentle Richard. He didn't enjoy causing anyone pain, but he would do what he needed to when necessary.

"Come," she said, looping her arm about his waist. "We need to get you home so we can get that leg taken care of."

Richard leaned heavily on Brynne, who steadied him as much as she could. They struggled for what seemed like hours, staggering through the ever-deepening snow. Between the drifts that were soon ankle deep and getting deeper, and Richard's nearly useless leg, they were making very slow progress.

"Brynne, leave me here. Go for help."

She was shaking her head before he had finished speaking. "If I leave you here, you'll die. We are almost there, we can make it."

She had a point. Richard made a renewed effort, helping to propel them forward as much as possible. He tried to keep as much of his weight as he could off her slender shoulders, but Brynne simply held tighter to his waist and the arm he'd draped across her shoulders. He risked a quick glance behind them and breathed a sigh of relief that whatever blood they were leaving was being rapidly covered, along with their footprints, by the still falling snow. As long as the bastards who'd attacked them weren't too close on their trail, they might have a good chance of escaping undetected.

After what felt like a lifetime, the welcoming glow of Brynne's townhouse came into view.

"Thank heavens," she whispered.

Richard snorted in agreement and together they stumbled up the steps. Brynne rang the bell while Richard banged on the door. It opened mid-bang and Richard sent up a quick prayer of thanks for Taggart's quick response. Brynne and Richard half dragged each other into the warmth of the house.

"Madam! Thank God you are all right." Taggart jumped forward and draped Richard's other arm over his shoulder, helping Brynne to get him inside. Once they were in with the door safely closed behind them, Richard brushed them both off.

"What happened, Taggart?" Richard asked, grunting as Brynne pulled the boot from his injured leg.

Taggart grimaced. "I'm afraid I'm not sure, sir."

Richard glowered, but his anger didn't seem to bother Taggart. "What do you mean, you're not sure?"

"They must have got the drop on me, sir. One minute I was keeping watch outside the window and the next thing I remember I was lying face down in the snow on the opposite side of the building. I made my way back to the window, but I didn't see any sign of you there. But there were footprints leading to the alley where we'd left the horses and the horses were gone. I assumed you'd left, had perhaps been running from whoever jumped me, so I made my way home as fast as I could only to find you hadn't arrived yet. I was about to head back out to look for you."

He did appear to have been interrupted as he'd been putting on extra layers for traveling outside. He wore his thick outdoor coat and had one glove on. And he was sporting a nicely blackening bruise on his right temple. Richard wasn't entirely convinced Taggart was telling the truth, but his story was plausible enough. And at the moment, Richard couldn't gather enough energy to care one way or the other. If the man was lying, Richard would take care of it later.

"I'll ready a guest bedroom, ma'am," Taggart said, giving Richard a pointed look before hurrying up the stairs to see to Richard's accommodations for the night.

"Come on," Brynne said, looping her arm back around his waist. He draped his arm over her shoulders, glad of the excuse to hold her close to him. She was stronger than she looked. While it was an obvious struggle for her to support his weight, she still managed, even as they began their slow ascent up the stairs. She never ceased to amaze him, this little spitfire that had wormed her way into his heart.

By the time they made it to the second floor, they were both panting. Brynne steered him into a guest bedroom where a cheery fire was beginning to crackle. Taggart tossed another log onto the flames and straightened.

"I'll have Mary bring up some hot tea and perhaps something to eat," Taggart said to Brynne.

"Thank you, Taggart. That would be lovely. Can you also have her bring some hot water?"

"Yes, ma'am."

He left without another glance at Richard.

"Not an admirer of mine, I see," Richard said.

Brynne shrugged, her eyes twinkling with amusement. "He's a bit protective of me. And I suspect he's a bit put out that he allowed those scoundrels to sneak up on him. He must have a dreadful headache. That would make anyone cranky."

"True." Richard smiled.

"I'm going to get out of these wet clothes. There should be a spare robe you can put on in the wardrobe." Brynne pointed to the armoire in the corner. "I'll…be back in a moment and we'll look at your leg."

She gazed at him for a moment, her mouth working as if she would say something more, before she turned on her heel and left. Richard stared after her, his eyes taking in every inch of her. The snow had molded her already indecently tight clothing even more to her shapely figure. He wanted nothing more than to follow her to her room, peel the wet clothing from her body, and spend the rest of the night warming her inch by inch. Repeatedly.

He drew in a jagged breath and went to the wardrobe. A thick robe hung there, along with a very warm looking pair of slippers. Richard ignored his pain and grabbed the robe and slippers. He removed his clothing as fast as possible, hissing as his wet trousers stuck a bit to the gash in his thigh. Luckily, it didn't look too deep and their journey through the snowstorm had helped reduce some of the swelling and blood loss. He would need to stitch it closed though.

He stood by the fire, warming himself as much as possible. A quiet knock sounded at his door and he drew the folds of the robe about him, tying it securely before he called "Come in."

Brynne entered, carrying what looked like a sewing kit. Two maids were behind her, one carrying a steaming kettle, the other a tray of tea and food. Thank heavens. He was starving. And the tea would go a long way toward warming him up. Then again, as he took in Brynne, who was wrapped in her own thick robe, her damp hair trailing down her back in a loose braid, a few hours alone with her might heat him up even more.

He shook his head. What kind of lecher was he to be lusting after a woman while he stood in her home bruised and bleeding?

"Sit," she commanded, pointing at a chair close to the fire.

Richard's lips twitched, but he followed her orders. She directed the maids where to put the trays they'd brought up and then dismissed them. They left, leaving the door open several inches in what he assumed was an effort at making the situation a bit more proper.

Richard's eyes widened in surprise when Brynne knelt at his feet and made to pull back the folds of his robe. He must have made some noise that she took for protest (though nothing could be farther from the truth) because she turned her impatient gaze to him and firmly grasped the edge of his robe. "I need to see how bad your leg is and stitch it if necessary."

He almost pointed out that he was the doctor and, as such, was fully capable of stitching himself up, but the sight of her pulling back his robe had him biting his tongue to keep the words from escaping. At the first tentative brush of her fingers along his thigh, he knew he'd gladly sport a hideous scar for the rest of his life before he'd stop her from touching him.

Brynne muttered something under her breath as she gently probed the gash. Richard sucked in his breath when she pressed along the edges of the wound.

"Sorry," she murmured. She sat back. "It definitely needs to be stitched." She went about gathering her supplies, Richard's surprise growing more and more as she got everything ready.

She lifted his leg a bit to put a folded towel beneath it and the movement caused his dressing gown to slide farther open, revealing much more of his anatomy than she'd expected to see.

Brynne froze, still supporting the weight of his thigh with one hand. Richard wondered if she even realized that she was staring at him since she made no move to cover him back up or look away. Far be it for him to disturb her enjoyment of the view he had to offer. Unfortunately, the leg she held began to throb and his involuntary hiss at the pain shooting up his thigh brought her back to her senses.

She flushed scarlet from the roots of her hair down to her neck and Richard couldn't hold back a satisfied chuckle as he pulled the robe back into its proper place. Brynne dropped his leg onto the towel, eliciting another gasp of pain from him. A smug smile briefly danced across her lips and Richard laughed again. He'd deserved that.

Brynne ignored him as she finished her preparations. She handed him a glass of whiskey. "Drink."

He didn't wait for her to tell him again. Already the flames of hell licked at his leg, and he knew once she started stitching the pain would only get worse. He forced two quick gulps, welcoming the fire burning down his throat.

She waited a moment, letting the liquor take some effect before she poured a healthy dose of it over his leg. A stream of fire hit his wound and he hissed. Brynne gently cleaned the area, her hands steady and quick.

"You really have a flare for this, don't you? Perhaps instead of letting you assist me, I should let you take over all the stitching that comes in," he said, watching as she held a needle over the flame of a candle. Once it had cooled, she plucked some thread from where she'd had it soaking in a bit of the alcohol and carefully threaded the needle.

"Well, my stitches *are* better than yours," she answered with a grin, not taking her attention from his leg.

The needle pierced his flesh and Richard gritted his teeth together. He kept his gaze riveted on Brynne's face, focusing on her instead of the dip and pull of the needle as she sewed his flesh back together. She bit at the corner of her bottom lip while she concentrated on her task. The urge to lean forward and nip at her tender flesh himself was nigh on irresistible. He closed his eyes to shut out the tempting sight. Maybe he'd do better to focus on the back of his eyelids until she'd finished.

It took an interminably long time.

At last, she snipped the thread with a dainty pair of sewing scissors. He looked down to admire her handiwork.

His eyebrows rose. "Very nice work. One of these days, you'll have to tell me where you learned to do that."

She grabbed a strip of clean linen and wrapped it about his leg. He sucked in his breath as her fingers gently skimmed his upper thigh.

"One of these days. Maybe," she said, carefully tying it off. She gathered her things and stood.

Richard chuckled.

Brynne rolled her eyes and deposited her sewing supplies before pouring him a cup of tea. "Drink this before it gets cold."

"Yes, ma'am."

• • •

Brynne sat in the chair opposite him and drank her own tea. She wasn't as collected as she hoped she appeared. The wound in his leg had been grave indeed. Truth be told, it was the glimpse she'd had of what lay beneath his robe that had her rattled. It had been a very long time since she'd seen a man unclothed. She ducked her head, hoping he hadn't seen the heat rising in her cheeks.

"So, where did you learn your stitching skills? You must have sewn a fair amount of wounds back together."

It took a moment for Brynne's brain to catch up with what Richard had been saying.

"It's not a skill most women of your station would be proficient at," he said.

Brynne snorted. "That's true enough. Things were a little different in California."

"Is it really such a wild place?"

"No, not all of it." Just the tiny town she'd lived in, the one her half-brother had terrorized so much that she and her sisters had had to become bandits in order to keep their ranch and their town from being destroyed.

"So who did you hone your skills on?"

"On myself, mostly."

His eyes widened again and Brynne smiled. She didn't want to spill her entire life story to him, but she couldn't help wanting to shock him either. It was too amusing to watch his eyebrows fly into his hairline whenever she'd make a comment such as that.

"Show me."

"I beg your pardon?" His simple command had her heart hammering in her chest.

"I'd like to see what I can expect from your handiwork. You said you'd had to stitch up your own wounds on occasion. Show me."

Brynne licked her suddenly dry lips. Then she caught the amused gleam in his eye. He either didn't believe her or didn't believe she'd show him. A slow smile spread over her lips. She could play this game as well as he.

She pulled the sleeve of her robe up to reveal a thin white scar that ran several inches down from her elbow. "I caught my arm on a broken piece of fencing we were mending."

Richard scooted forward in his chair to get a good look and took her arm in his hands, twisting it gently to catch the firelight. "Very nice work," he said.

"Thank you." She put her foot up on the chair beside his leg, her smile widening when he froze. She pulled the robe up a bit, enough to reveal the spot on her ankle where she had a small scar.

"My horse was spooked by a snake and he reared. I fell and landed on a rock."

Richard reached out, his hand encircling her ankle. Brynne's heart pounded.

"That must have hurt." His fingers trailed over the scar, lightly brushing her skin.

"Yes," she murmured, unable to make her voice work while his hand trailed slowly up her leg. When he reached her calf she pulled from his grasp and took several steps back, but Richard stood and followed her. She kept backing up, heading for the door.

"What about that one?" he asked, pointing at her shoulder.

"Which one?" she asked, already knowing which one he meant. Her back hit the edge of the door, forcing her to stop.

Richard trailed a finger along the scar that poked out from the neckline of her robe. "This one."

"Oh." Brynne tried to keep her breathing slow and even but couldn't seem to catch her breath. "My sister mended that one. Couldn't reach it myself."

Richard laughed, though it was different than before. Still amused, yes. But with an intense undertone that hadn't been there before.

"Talented family." He reached behind her and slowly pushed the door closed. Brynne kept her back pressed to the wood, walking backwards until the door clicked into place and she was trapped between it and Richard's arms. He braced a hand on either side of her and leaned in, brushing his lips against hers.

Brynne's head swam and, for a moment, she let herself be carried away on the wave of sensation that Richard was creating as his lips moved over hers. She knew she couldn't let him continue.

She turned her face. "Richard," she breathed. She leaned her forehead against the arm that kept her imprisoned while his lips continued their path over her cheek and neck. "Richard, we shouldn't."

Brynne ducked under his arm, but Richard caught her about the waist. "No more running," he said, drawing her back into his arms, pressing her back to his chest.

He kissed her cheek, the sensitive spot under her ear, and trailed his lips down her neck. She hesitated only a second more and then, with a small groan of surrender, she turned in his arms and leaned in to kiss him back. Her lips met his with a desperation that had been building between them for months. All the looks, the small touches, and the stolen kisses, erupted in a fireball of passion that she was sure would consume them both.

Brynne wrapped her arms around Richard's neck, her hands tangling in his hair, keeping his mouth molded to hers. He scooped her up and carried her to the bed, not breaking the kiss as he laid her down and stretched out beside her. Her fingers pulled at the ties of his robe and he tore himself away from her only long enough to divest them both of their clothing.

For a moment, he gazed down at her, speechless at the gift she was offering. "You are so unbelievably beautiful."

She reached up for him, made more confident by the desire she saw in his eyes. "Come here."

He was more than happy to oblige.

Chapter Eighteen

Brynne squinted against the brilliant light filtering in through a crack in the drapes. With a groan, she rolled over and tucked herself into Richard's side, sighing when he pulled her tight against him and kissed her head. He wrapped his arms about her and drew her further into the blankets.

She wondered if the snow had melted enough yet for him to leave and found herself fervently hoping that wasn't the case. The morning after their heist, they'd awoken to find the snow so deep they couldn't get through the door. Richard said he couldn't remember a time when it had snowed so much in one night in Boston. And then he'd taken her back to bed and proven what a blessing being snowed in could be. That had been four days ago, and they'd barely left her rooms since then.

Taggart had taken to leaving their meals outside her door and the rest of the staff seemed to have made an agreement to leave the lovers in peace unless they expressly called for something. Which they rarely did. They spent nearly every waking minute reveling in each other.

Brynne burrowed into Richard, burying her face into his neck. He cringed a bit and chuckled. She kissed him under his jaw line, loving that he was ticklish. He growled and rolled her onto her back, putting her lips to much better use.

Brynne was still amazed at how her body responded so completely to Richard's touch. She'd only had a month with Jake before he'd disappeared. Hardly enough time to learn all the ways one could love. She still had much to learn about the more physical aspects of loving someone. And Richard was only too happy to teach her.

They were both content to take it slow this time, lingering to explore each other, over and over, until there wasn't a coherent thought left in Brynne's head. Afterwards, they lay together, Richard's words floating over her in a pleasant haze.

His soft chuckle caught her attention and she looked up at him.

"You haven't heard a word I said, have you?"

Brynne gave him a lazy smile. "I heard all of them," she insisted. "I'm not sure how many actually sank in."

Richard laughed again and gave her a lingering kiss. "I was saying that if you preferred not to live at the clinic after the wedding, then we can start looking for another home. I would prefer a place a little closer to the clinic than this house is, if you are amenable. However, I know it might be more comfortable for Coraline if we lived here since she is already settled in and if you preferred to stay here, I'll abide by your choice. If you are open to moving, however, that would be wonderful as I'll still need to spend a considerable amount of time at the clinic until I can find someone to help me. But I am more than happy to do whatever you feel is best for you and Coraline."

Richard's words finally sank in and Brynne sat up, clutching the sheet to her chest. "Richard, slow down. What are you talking about? What wedding?"

Richard frowned. "Our wedding."

Brynne's heart skipped several beats and for a split second, she let the exhilaration at the idea of being Richard's wife flow through her. But the initial jolt of happiness faded quickly. It hadn't been some declaration of undying love. It hadn't even been a proposal. He was making plans for their entire future and hadn't even bothered to ask her about it first.

Brynne opened her mouth to respond but froze, not wanting to say the wrong thing. Overbearing or not, the man wanted to marry her and that wasn't something she took lightly.

"Richard, why do you think we are getting married?"

He frowned, his forehead crinkling in confusion. "But of course we must get married. My darling, I've spent the last four days in your bed. A fact we may be able to keep quiet for a time, but we certainly need to be married as soon as possible."

Brynne's happiness faded. "You want to marry me to protect your good name."

"No." He took her face in his hands. "To protect you."

Brynne pulled away from him. It wasn't a bad reason, really. She was sure there were plenty of men who wanted to marry her for less selfless reasons. Still, she was nobody's charity mission.

"That's very kind of you, Richard. But I assure you, it isn't necessary."

"Of course it's necessary. What if you're with child?"

The image of a baby, one with Richard's gorgeous blue eyes and adorable dimple, made her falter. But only for a moment.

"That's unlikely." She rose from the bed and grabbed her robe from the floor. Their little haven had been ruined.

"Brynne? Have I said something wrong?"

Brynne pulled her robe about her and shoved her feet in her slippers.

"Brynne?"

A knock sounded at the door and Brynne breathed a sigh of relief for the temporary reprieve. She waited a moment while Richard got up and pulled on some clothes and then opened the door. A flustered Mary stood in the hallway.

"Begging your pardon, ma'am. But I'm not sure what to do and I thought I should let you know right away."

"Let me know what, Mary?"

"It's Mr. Taggart, ma'am. He's…." Richard came to stand by Brynne. Mary flushed scarlet and turned her gaze to the floor.

"Mary?" Brynne prompted. "What about Taggart?"

"He's gone, ma'am. He's nowhere to be found."

"Gone?"

Brynne looked at Richard and saw her concern mirrored on his face.

"Did he leave any word? A note? Anything?" Richard asked.

The girl flushed beet red again and wouldn't meet Richard's eyes. "No, sir. And when there was no sign of him this morning, we checked his room. His belongings are gone."

"Does any of the staff know why he'd leave? Have there been any problems?"

"No ma'am, at least none that I know of. He did get a letter two days ago. It upset him something fierce. He went out for a bit and when he came back, he was right as rain again. I didn't think anything of it until this morning when he just upped and vanished."

"All right, thank you Mary," Brynne said, trying to keep her unease from her voice. Why in heaven's name would Taggart disappear with no word? A ball of worry gnawed at her gut. Taggart knew too many of her secrets. She could only hope, as uncharitable as it was, that his reason for leaving had to do with one of his own countless secrets, rather than with hers.

"Please send Beth to me."

Mary shuffled her feet. "Well that's the other thing, ma'am. Beth left a couple days ago."

"What? Why did no one tell me?"

"Mr. Taggart said as how we weren't to disturb you; that he'd take care of it."

"Why did she leave?"

Mary's blush deepened to such a severe degree that Brynne feared she'd take ill. "Begging your pardon ma'am, but she said…well, she said that she couldn't abide working in a house…well, that is, working for a woman who…" Her eyes flashed to Richard and she appeared close to tears.

No matter. Brynne knew exactly why Beth had left. "It's all right, Mary. Don't trouble yourself." She patted the poor girl's arm.

Mary took a deep breath and squared her shoulders. "The rest of the staff don't feel that way, ma'am. We think you're a good mistress, and as long as you're happy and what you're doin' don't harm no one, well…that's all right in our book."

Brynne smiled, knowing it had taken a great deal of courage for the girl to have spoken as she had. "Thank you, Mary. Give me a few moments and I'll be down and we'll get this whole mess sorted out."

"Yes, ma'am." Mary hurried off with a relieved smile.

Brynne turned around to find Richard regarding her with a grim countenance. "Do you still wonder why I insist we marry? It will only get worse, Brynne."

Brynne pushed past him and gathered her undergarments. "We'll discuss it later."

"Brynne…"

She held up her hand. "Later, Richard. We need to find

out what is going on first." If he continued to harp on the subject, she was going to lose the tenuous hold she had on her emotions.

Richard looked like was going to argue but instead he held out his hand for her crinoline and corset. She hesitated for a moment but as lacing herself into everything would prove difficult and Beth wasn't around to do it, she needed his help. He helped her into her hoops and corset and tightened the stays with surprisingly expert fingers. Brynne didn't want to dwell on why he knew his way around women's undergarments. She had enough to occupy her mind without adding that.

The fact that Beth had run off hurt more than Brynne wanted to admit. She'd assumed she and the maid had a decent relationship and the maid had certainly considered Richard the catch of the century. Perhaps it didn't count if one bypassed social protocol and enjoyed the benefits of marriage without the actual wedding. And if Beth felt strongly enough about it to leave Brynne's service over it, then it was only a matter of time before half the town knew that Richard had spent four days in her bed.

Four wonderful, heart-pounding, unforgettable days.

Brynne sighed. All she had to do was agree to marry him and she could relive the last four days every day for the rest of her life. There would be a hint of scandal about their hasty nuptials, but it would soon blow over. And many couples married for far less reason. At least she and Richard were… compatible. Her cheeks warmed with the memory of exactly how compatible they were. And she knew he cared for her. Was it wrong to want more?

Richard finished lacing her up and helped her get her skirt and petticoats on. For some reason, watching him pull the material over her body and arrange the folds of fabric stirred the fire in her blood almost as much as it had when he'd been *removing* her clothing. He held out her bodice, letting his fingers brush across her skin as he helped her draw it across her shoulders. Her breath hitched in her throat and the hands that reached up to button the material shook. Richard pushed them aside, smiling down at her as he took over. He carefully arranged the small lace collar at her throat and ran his hands down her ribcage to her waist, smoothing the form-fitting silk.

Brynne's lips parted, her whole body yearning for him. If he were to ask her again, she'd say yes. She'd say yes to anything that allowed her to be with him morning, noon, and night. She might regret it later, but at the moment she was having a hard time giving a damn.

With a deep breath and more willpower than she'd ever had to exert in her life, Brynne took a step back. Richard let his hands fall, watching her as she retreated to her vanity table. When she picked up her heavy silver brush and attacked her hair, he turned and gathered his own clothing, dressing hastily while she wrestled her thick mop into some semblance of a simple but proper bun at the nape of her neck. The process might have gone smoother if she hadn't kept getting glimpses of Richard in her mirror. It seemed a shame to cover such a beautiful body with clothing…

Brynne pushed aside the tumultuous thoughts. First things first. Even more troublesome than Beth leaving was Taggart's disappearance.

"Why do you think Taggart left?" Brynne asked, desperate to both break the silence and to erase the images in her mind.

"I've been running over a few possibilities, and none of them are good."

"Such as?"

"Well, we'll need to ask the staff if there is anything missing. If there's not, that would rule out thievery."

"I can't see him stealing from me. He was Jake's friend."

"Yes, which makes it all the more strange that he would

disappear without a word."

"Do you think it has something to do with our little excursion the other night?"

Richard frowned. "Considering how willingly helpful he was, I think not."

A steady throbbing took up residence at Brynne's temples and she closed her eyes and massaged her head. Richard gathered her in his arms and kissed her forehead.

"We'll find out what's going on, I promise."

Brynne let him hold her for a moment, wishing she could stay wrapped in his arms forever. But as Cilla would say, wishes were about as useful as a skunk in a flower bed. The thought of her tough-as-nails sister brought a smile to Brynne's lips and an extra dose of courage to her heart.

"All right," she said, pulling away from Richard, "let us go find out what is amiss in this crazy household."

Richard opened the door for her and let her lead the way.

. . .

Brynne thoroughly questioned each member of the household, trying to find any clue as to why Taggart had left. But Richard's mind was only half on the mystery of the butler's disappearance. To be perfectly honest, he didn't care two wits why the man had left, as long as the reason wasn't something that could hurt Brynne. What he did care about was why the stubborn woman was refusing to marry him. Had the last four days meant nothing to her? He could have sworn that their time together had meant as much to her as it had to him. They hadn't been merely two people finding pleasure in one another (though there had been *plenty* of pleasure to be had). They had been two people really and truly making love to one another.

All the tender moments, the murmured declarations of

love, the — Richard froze.

He knew he'd told her over and over that he loved her while they'd made love. But had he said it when he'd asked her to marry him?

Oh, for the love of all that was holy. If he hadn't been standing in a hall full of jittery servants, he'd have turned to the marble column he was leaning on and struck his head against it a few times.

He hadn't asked her to marry him. He'd *told* her they were getting married. And he hadn't even managed to give her a good reason, like because he was so madly in love with her he couldn't bear being apart from her ever again. Oh no. He'd told her it was so the hellhound society women wouldn't gossip. Of all the stupid, pig-headed, brainless —

No wonder she'd flat out refused him. It was a miracle she hadn't tossed him out on his undeserving derriere.

Well. He might not be able to bring back her maid or solve the mystery of the missing butler, but there was one wrong in her life he could right. And he was going to do it immediately.

He marched over to her and interrupted her mid-sentence. "Brynne, I need to have a word with you."

She looked up at him, her eyes rounding with surprise. "I'm sorry, Richard, can it wait a moment?"

"I'm sorry, I'm afraid this can't wait."

He took her by the elbow, ignoring her little squeak of protest, and steered her into the study, closing the door behind them.

"Richard, what on earth —"

He took her face in his hands and kissed her, letting every ounce of love and passion that he felt for her wash over them. When she was trembling in his arms, he pulled away just far enough so he could look into her eyes.

"Brynne Richardson Forrester, I love you more than I will ever be able to adequately express. Until you came into my life, I didn't even know that it was possible for me to feel so deeply for a woman. I would gladly lay my life down for you. You already own my heart. You and Coraline have brought me more love and contentment than I ever knew was possible. I want you both in my life. I *need* you in my life. I know I made a terrible botch of it before, and for that I ought to be horse-whipped. I can only beg your forgiveness for my terrible lapse in judgment.

"If you would do me the supreme honor of being my wife, I swear to you I will spend every day of the rest of my life showing you how much I love you."

Two fat tears rolled down Brynne's cheeks as she smiled up at him. His heart thumped at the sight. He'd gladly give everything he owned to keep that smile on her face. He wiped her tears away with his thumbs.

"Will you marry me?"

Brynne nodded. "Yes, Richard. I would be honored to be your wife."

Richard wrapped his arms about her waist and spun her around, her laughter joining his as she clung to his arms. He set her down and kissed her again.

"Let's send for Coraline in the morning. I want our family to be together as soon as possible."

"Oh, Richard. I love you so much."

He took her hand and led her back out to where the staff still waited. He didn't care why the damn butler had left. Nothing had been stolen. And truth be told, Richard had never been comfortable with him in Brynne's household, anyway. Good riddance, as far as Richard was concerned. But Brynne cared, and so he would support her in finding the man if that's what she wished.

They sent a letter off to Lucy the very next morning, asking her to bring Coraline home.

But before the letter had a chance to reach her, Lucy was

on their doorstep. Without Coraline.

The first words out of her mouth had Richard's heart sinking into his gut.

"Is she here? Do you have Coraline?"

"What do you mean, is she here?" Brynne shrieked. "Where is my baby?"

Lucy's already pale face went so white her lips were nearly invisible. "I don't know," she muttered. "Dear God, I don't know where she is."

Chapter Nineteen

Brynne heard Lucy's voice from a distance, as if there were cotton stuffing her ears. She could see Lucy's mouth moving, but she couldn't focus on her sister's face. Everything seemed muffled, blurry. Richard shouted. Lunged toward her. And then she was looking at the ceiling and Richard bending over her.

"Did I faint?" she asked.

"For a moment. How are you feeling?"

"Get me up."

Richard pulled her to her feet, keeping his arm about her waist. She didn't bother stepping away. She needed his support. The thought of her baby missing…blackness licked at the edges of her vision again and she shook it off with a ferocious impatience. Being insensible wouldn't help find Coraline.

"Let's go into the study and we can figure out what's going on," Richard suggested.

"Shall I bring in some tea?" Mary asked. She didn't wait for confirmation, but rushed off to the kitchens.

"Tea," Richard snorted. He led Brynne into the study, deposited her in a chair, and went straight for the brandy decanter. He poured two glasses and handed one to Brynne before knocking back a healthy swallow of his own.

"I'm so sorry, Brynne. I don't know what happened." Lucy dropped to the floor at her sister's side and laid her head on Brynne's lap, her body wracked with sobs.

"Shhh," Brynne murmured, smoothing back her hair. "Just tell us. Please."

Lucy made a heroic effort to pull herself together. She sat next to Brynne, her hands kneading at the folds of her dress.

"It was Finn…Mr. Taggart. He came to fetch us."

"What?" Ice ran through Brynne's veins, making every breath she drew fresh agony. Her gaze shot to Richard, whose own eyes were narrowing with anger. The vein at his temple was pulsing and Brynne could see the joint of his jaw popping in and out as he clenched his teeth.

"What do you mean Taggart came to fetch you. I didn't send him."

"Oh no, no, no!" Lucy buried her face in her hands, her whole body seeming to shrink in on itself.

"Lucy, tell us exactly what happened," Richard said, his voice gentle but firmly insistent.

Lucy took a few deep breaths. "Two days ago, he arrived at the farm, said that you'd sent for us and wanted us to come as soon as possible and that he had train tickets for first thing the next morning and would escort us home. I didn't let her out of my sight. She was by my side until we got on the train. But…" The tears welled in her eyes again and her lower lip trembled.

Brynne could scarcely breathe. *What had happened to her sweet baby?*

"Lucy," Richard prompted.

"I was so tired. I'd been up very late the night before. It

had been such a long time since I'd seen Finn…Mr. Taggart… and we got to visiting and lost track of time. And the train left so early. Coraline wanted to explore, but I wanted to get settled in. Mr. Taggart offered to show her around the train while I rested. I didn't see any reason why I shouldn't trust him. He'd been alone with her before. He'd taken us on excursions. I never dreamed…"

Brynne patted her sister's hand, but inside she was screaming. Part of her wanted to berate Lucy for being so naïve, so trustingly stupid, so blinded by her infatuation with the butler that she'd willingly put Coraline in danger.

But deep down, Brynne knew none of that was true. Lucy would never have put Coraline in harm's way. They'd all trusted Taggart. Brynne herself most likely would have done the same thing. It wasn't Lucy's fault. It was Taggart's. And if she ever got her hands on the man again…if anything happened to Coraline…

"Continue, please, Lucy." Richard hadn't moved from the spot where he stood near their chairs. His body was so taut with tension Brynne was afraid to touch him. He was too controlled, too calm. And Brynne knew it was all a cover for what seethed under the surface. She could see the rage and fear in his eyes. He'd never looked so dangerous. It almost frightened her.

"I fell asleep," Lucy said, her voice barely audible. "Not for long, only a few minutes. But by the time I awoke, the train had already left the station. And Coraline and Mr. Taggart weren't back yet. I raised the alarm immediately. I had them search the entire train and when they were nowhere to be found, I wasn't sure what I should do. I thought of going back to the station, but then what if they were on the train but had been missed? Or what if they'd gotten on a different train and were on their way home?

I got off at the next stop and wired the station in Maryland, asked them to conduct a search. If they found Coraline and Mr. Taggart, they were to wire ahead to the Boston station. But when I arrived here, their telegram stated that no one had seen them. The later train to Boston won't arrive for another few hours. They might be on that…but…"

Brynne looked at Richard, a faint hope sparking in her heart. Maybe they'd gotten off to look at the outside of the train and hadn't been able to re-board. They could have boarded the later train. They could be on their way to Boston at that very moment. Richard's hooded eyes met Brynne's briefly and he shook his head slightly.

There was no reason for Taggart to take Coraline off the train unless he planned on abducting her. And if he had intentionally run off with her, the last thing he'd do would be to board a train to Boston. It would be too easy for them to lie in wait at the station and discover them as they disembarked.

"What do we do?" Brynne asked, for the first time in her life feeling utterly helpless.

Richard went over to her and knelt down. He brushed a thumb across her cheek and let his hand trail down to her shoulder. He gave it a gentle squeeze.

"We'll go to the train station, to be certain they aren't on that train. And then…I think we must go to the police."

If he'd plunged a knife through her heart, Brynne didn't think she'd hurt as badly. If Coraline was lost to her forever, she didn't think she'd be able to go on. Losing Jake had shattered her heart. Losing Coraline…she'd never recover. It would obliterate her soul.

• • •

They weren't on the next train. Or the one after that. No telegrams arrived.

Brynne and Richard came back to the house and Brynne

slumped on the sofa in front of the fireplace. Richard sat beside her and drew her into his arms.

"What do we do now, Richard? Where is she?"

"We'll find her. I promise you."

Brynne looked into his worried eyes and uttered the one word that filled her with despair. "How?"

Richard didn't answer. He didn't know how they were going to get Coraline back any more than Brynne did. He leaned forward and pressed a kiss to her forehead.

"I think it's time we contact the authorities."

Brynne nodded, though she had no idea how they would be able to find her little girl.

A gentle knock sounded at the door and Mary entered.

"Excuse me, ma'am, but this was just delivered for you." She held out a small note on the silver platter that Taggart had always used for the mail.

Brynne took it and murmured thanks. The envelope had MRS. FORRESTER printed on the front, but no other information. Brynne opened it and cried out. She slapped a hand over her mouth to keep from howling, her body trembling from the effort.

"What is it?" Richard asked, his face paling in alarm.

Brynne upturned the envelope, spilling a small gold locket on a delicate chain into her hand. *Her* locket, the one Coraline had taken to wearing. Brynne squeezed it tight in her fist and ripped the envelope apart in her haste to remove the note.

Each word printed on the parchment sent a stab of fear and anguish straight through her heart.

Brynne handed Richard the paper. Someone with a heavy hand had meticulously printed out the short note.

WE HAVE YOUR DAUGHTER. CONTACT NO ONE. WAIT FOR INSTRUCTIONS.

That was it. Nothing more. Nothing on where she was,

how she was doing, who had her, what they wanted.

It was maddening.

"Mary, who delivered this?" Richard asked.

"No one, sir. The bell at the door rang but when I answered it, there was no one there. Just that note under a rock on the stoop."

"How long ago?"

"Just this minute, sir."

Richard jumped up and ran from the room. Brynne followed, waiting at the front door as Richard ran outside and stopped passersby, gesturing to their door as he questioned everyone he could.

But it was to no avail. No one had seen anyone leaving anything on their doorstep. They went back into the house, Brynne's body sagging in defeat.

"Well. At least we know what's happened," Richard said, his voice dangerously low. "And we can prepare."

"How?"

"They'll want to ransom her. If they'd meant to harm her, we'd have never heard from them. If they are telling us to contact no one, they don't want the authorities involved. They'll send instructions for where to meet them, and how much they want."

"But how do we know she's unharmed? They could be doing anything to her. She could be cold, or hungry, or hurt."

"She's no good to them if she's harmed. They'll take care of her so they can get their money."

Lucy, who'd barely said a word since she'd arrived home, finally spoke up. "I don't think Finn will let any harm come to her."

Brynne couldn't contain her emotions any longer. Hearing Lucy defend Taggart after all he'd done was more than she could take. She surged to her feet, rounding on her sister with a fury so strong her head swam.

"Your precious *Finn* is the one who took her! He's already harmed her. He's stolen my baby! How can you think well of him?"

Lucy cringed, drawing in upon herself as if making herself smaller would shield her from her sister's wrath. "I know he's responsible for this. And I don't know why he did it. But I know him, Brynne. I *know* him. He won't hurt her."

Brynne's chest burned with the rage that was beginning to eat her alive. She prayed with every ounce of her being that Coraline was returned to her. Because she was very much afraid that if she wasn't, if her baby was lost to her forever or was in some way irreparably harmed, she'd never be able to forgive her sister. She knew how unfair that thought was, but she couldn't keep it from festering in her mind.

She couldn't bring herself to respond to Lucy's remarks. She didn't trust what would come out and some still sane part of her didn't want to say anything that she'd later regret.

Richard, heaven bless him, came to her rescue. He stood and wrapped his arms about her. She grabbed the lapels of his jacket and buried her face against his chest, breathing in the scent of him. He was her haven, the only place she felt safe.

He held her tight and kissed the top of her head. "All we can do is wait and see what they want. I don't think we'll have to wait long. The longer they drag this out, the more danger they are in of being caught. They'll want this to be over as much as we do."

Brynne took a deep breath and prayed that he was right.

Chapter Twenty

Richard was thankful when his words proved to be true. Within a few hours, another note was delivered. This time, they were waiting. Richard had positioned Mary by the back entrance with instructions to watch the windows for anyone approaching the door. And he took up position at the front door. They'd get some answers this time.

When a young boy ran up the steps, a note clutched in his hand, Richard had the door open, and had yanked the poor boy inside before he could knock.

Richard snatched the note out of his hand. "Who gave this to you?"

The boy twisted in Richard's grip. "It weren't no one, just a man. He paid me real good to bring it here, said to leave it under the rock on the doorstep."

"What did he look like? Where did he find you?"

"Hey, leave off," he said, pushing at Richard's hand. "Let me go if you want me to talk."

Richard frowned but let the boy go, taking care to stand in front of the door so the mongrel couldn't escape.

"Talk."

Now that the boy was no longer being threatened with bodily harm, a bit of the fear had drained away. He crossed his arms with a cocky grin. "He gave me a whole dollar to deliver that note and to say nothing about it. Doesn't seem right to break that agreement."

Richard took a deep breath, trying to calm the fury threatening to break through. The kid was filthy, scrawny, and was obviously used to surviving on his wits and whatever he could con out of people. The child had no way of knowing what was going on and would probably be rightly more interested in his own survival if he did.

"I'll triple whatever he paid you."

The boy's eyes nearly bugged out of his head. "It was in Haymarket Square. I don't know who the man was, he seemed a regular sort of fellow. Not dressed real fancy, but not like the likes of me either."

"Did he have any marks on his face? Anything about him that was out of the ordinary?"

"No, sir. Nothing different about him at all. Couldn't pick him out of a crowd to save my life, I reckon."

Not Taggart then. His face would definitely have been one the boy remembered. Which meant that Taggart wasn't working alone. And that made things considerably more complicated.

Richard dug three dollar coins out of his pocket and dropped them into the boy's eager hand. And then he added a ten dollar bill. "If you see the man again, follow him. Don't let yourself be seen. Don't put yourself in any danger. But I want to know as much about him as you can find out."

"Yes, sir!"

Richard opened the door and the boy scampered off with an ear-splitting grin. Brynne came out from the parlor.

"We'll probably never see him again."

Richard shrugged. "If not, at least the boy will be able to keep himself fed for a while. But I have a feeling he'll do his best to find out as much as he can. After all, if we were willing to pay that much up front, he'll be pretty sure we'll pay even more to get the information out of him."

A ghost of a smile touched Brynne's lips, but quickly faded. Richard went to her, his heart aching at the sight of her haunted, pale face. He gave her a quick kiss and then opened the note which was once again addressed to Mrs. Forrester.

COME TO THE COMMON AT MIDNIGHT. $10,000.00.
TELL NO ONE. COME ALONE.

Brynne leaned against him.

"Do you have that much?"

Brynne nodded.

"If it will be a hardship, I have some—"

"It won't be a hardship."

Richard's brows furrowed. It was an enormous amount of money. He'd known, of course, that Brynne was wealthy. But still, that amount would leave a sizable dent in even his substantial fortune.

"Well, at least I know you aren't marrying me for my money, since you don't appear to realize how much I've got," she said, her eyes twinkling with genuine amusement for the first time since this whole nightmare had begun.

He stroked her cheek and pulled her in close. "I wouldn't care if you were a penniless beggar on the street." He kissed her, exploring her mouth until she began making the little noises that he loved so much. His heart lightened a bit at the little moan of protest she made when he released her.

"We'd better get to the bank. It might take a while to withdraw such an amount."

"No need," Brynne said, pulling out of his arms. She led

him to the library and closed the door behind them, taking care to draw the bolt. Then she went round to each window and drew the drapes. The room would have been plunged into darkness save for the twin windows set high in the walls that overlooked the back gardens.

"Follow me."

Richard obeyed, wondering where she was taking him. Surely she couldn't have that much money hidden in the house. She stopped in front of one of the bookcases and pushed on it. The case swung open to reveal a small room. Inside, the room curved into a small alcove, the mahogany walls carved floor to ceiling with an incredible relief of a large tree, its branches encircling the room, each leaf and twig exquisitely carved into the wood. The room was empty save for a bench on either side of the carved trunk of the tree.

"It's stunning," Richard said, at a loss for any other words to describe the incredible room.

"It is. There were several reasons I choose this home over one in the more fashionable neighborhoods," she said. "One of those reasons was because the previous owner was a bit on the eccentric and secretive side. He made several alterations that were appealing to me. This is one of them."

She went to the relief, to where a large owl had been carved sitting in a recessed hollow in the middle of the trunk. Brynne grasped the left edge of the branch forming the carved hollow and pulled it toward her. It swung open to reveal a small safe.

"Good gracious," Richard said before he could stop himself. He'd seen hidden safes before, naturally. In fact, he had one himself in his own home. But he'd never seen one so elaborate.

Brynne twisted the dial as she entered the combination and pulled open the safe to reveal a small stack of documents, a few items of jewelry, and more money than Richard had ever seen in one place before. Brynne removed what she needed, leaving behind only one small stack, and closed the safe, sealing it once again behind its façade.

"Why do you keep so much in your home?" Richard asked. He kept a decent amount of money in his house as well. It was convenient to keep a certain amount on hand so one didn't have to run to the bank whenever a bit of currency was needed. But she had a fortune hidden behind that tree.

"I find it more convenient than having to make a withdrawal or having someone from the bank bring me funds whenever I need them. And I'm not used to relying on a bank to control my money. I don't trust them much," she said with a shrug.

Having met some of the bankers in town, he couldn't say that he faulted her. Especially after the panic from the year before. He followed her out of the alcove and pulled the door closed behind them. Brynne went to a small writing desk in the corner of the room and grabbed a book that rested there. She opened it, revealing its false center; a clever way to keep trinkets and odds and ends nearby without cluttering up one's space. She upended it, sprinkling its contents across the desk, and layered the money inside.

"Now, we wait," she said, her forlorn tone making Richard's heart clench.

"We'll get her back, my love," he promised. "And then we'll make Taggart and his associates pay."

For the first time since Coraline had gone missing, a genuine smile crossed Brynne's lips.

• • •

Waiting for midnight to approach was the hardest thing Brynne had ever had to do. She sat in the study, watching the second hand of the clock slowly tick by. She knew watching it only made the time go by more slowly...

Tick.

But she couldn't make herself do anything else.

Tick.

Richard and Lucy had left at ten o'clock to take up their positions. Despite what the note said, they had no intention of Brynne arriving alone. They would make certain that her back was covered. And if at all possible, they would make certain the kidnappers didn't get away with what they had done.

Tick.

The money didn't matter to Brynne. They could have it.

Tick.

But they had taken her daughter. That she would never forgive.

Tick.

For that she would follow them to the ends of the earth.

Tick.

The clock struck the half hour. Eleven thirty.

Brynne stood, gathered her book full of money, and strode to the front door. The weight of the gun strapped to her ankle, the one in the pocket of her skirt, and the knife in its sheath at the small of her back gave her confidence as she strode toward the door. She wished she could face her enemies unencumbered by skirts. She needed her limbs free so she could fight. But Richard convinced her that their best bet at the element of surprise was if all appeared as normal as possible. Showing up dressed like a male gunslinger might scare off their prey.

And alerting any innocent passersby that something was going on wouldn't be wise either. The last thing they wanted was for anyone to find them interesting enough to pay attention to what they were doing. Brynne cared less than a two-headed pig about what people might think of her clothing choice. But Richard had a point on the rest. Alerting

Taggart and his cronies that she was there to fight wasn't the smart thing to do.

The one concession she'd made to her own comfort was the absence of a corset. The ridiculous skirts were one thing; at least the hoops kept them from tangling around her legs. If she couldn't give all her limbs freedom, she'd at least ensure that she could breathe.

She did, however, don the leather gloves she'd worn on the ranch. They slipped onto her fingers, the familiar leather molding to her skin. They still smelled of California; a tang of horse and the outdoors that hit Brynne with a wave of homesickness so strong she had to hold her breath for a moment. They never should have left. If they had stayed where they belonged, Coraline wouldn't be in danger now. But then, Brynne would have never met Richard. The thought of never having known him was almost physically painful. But even that she'd gladly suffer if it meant her baby would be safe.

Brynne nodded her thanks to Mary and turned to leave.

"I'll have the little one's bed all ready for her when you bring her home," Mary said.

Brynne choked back the tears that burned at the back of her throat. "Thank you, Mary." The girl's kindness and belief gave Brynne strength. She marched into the night to rescue her daughter.

Chapter Twenty-One

Brynne arrived at the deserted gazebo a few minutes early. There was always something going on in the park, but at this end, so late at night, there was no one about. A perfect place for a ransom exchange.

Brynne's eyes strained to see in the darkness. She couldn't make out much. The moon was full, but the abundance of shrubbery and the clouds that kept passing across its surface created pockets of inky blackness that no amount of staring would penetrate. All she could hear were the distant sounds of other park-goers enjoying their festivities, an occasional hoot of an owl. She knew Richard and Lucy were hidden in the darkness beyond the gazebo. She longed for some sign from them but knew that any sound they made would betray their presence and position.

So she waited. It was almost time. A few minutes more.

A rustling sound drew her attention to her left.

Finnegan Taggart stepped out from a cluster of large bushes. He didn't come out all the way, but kept his back nearly touching the shrubs. Brynne didn't wait for instructions. If he wasn't going to come to her, she sure as hell would go to him.

He met her gaze, not flinching or wavering as she stalked toward him. He didn't seem to fear her at all. There were no weapons in his hands. Good.

Brynne marched up to him and swung, her fist connecting with his face before he had a chance to blink. She hit him hard enough to make his head snap back, hard enough to make her hand throb in protest. Perhaps not the wisest course of action. It was her gun hand. But striking the son of a bitch had been immensely satisfying.

Taggart massaged his jaw, but he didn't retaliate. He didn't even look angry. Just resigned.

Enough of this!

"Where is my daughter?"

"Where is the money?"

Brynne sneered, letting every ounce of the contempt and disgust she felt for him show on her face. "I have it. But I'm not handing it over until I see my daughter."

Taggart nodded as if he'd expected that and turned his head toward the bushes. He whistled three sharp notes and then, before Brynne could register his intent to move, he stood toe to toe with her. He grasped her arm to pull her nearer and whispered in her ear.

"I had no choice in this. I did the best I could for you and your family, I swear it."

Brynne glared, shoving his hand off her arm. "By stealing my daughter?"

"It would have gone far worse for her if I hadn't been the one to do it," he whispered urgently.

A twig snapped and the bushes parted to reveal a scruffy man with a sneer on his face and an evil gleam in his eyes. His hand gripped Coraline's shoulder tightly.

"Momma!" Coraline tried to run to her, but the man hauled her back.

It took every ounce of self-control she had and some that God must have lent her, to keep from running to her daughter. She had to keep her wits about her, had to do this right.

"Hi, chickabiddy. It'll be okay. Momma needs to talk to these men for a minute."

"The money," Taggart said.

Brynne went back to the gazebo and retrieved the book from where she'd stowed it under a bench. She shoved it into Taggart's waiting hands, her breath coming in short, seething bursts. She tried to calm down, slow her heart rate. If she didn't gain some control, these blackguards would get the best of her.

Taggart flipped open the book and quickly flipped through the stacked bills. "It's all here," he said to his associate.

"Good. Then I guess we'll be going." He backed into the bushes, and took Coraline with him.

"My daughter," Brynne said, fear squeezing her heart in a vice-like grip that nearly brought her to her knees.

Taggart turned to the thin man with a confused frown. "She paid the ransom. Let the little girl go."

"Well, mate, we have a small problem with that. They've both seen our faces now. Can't have them running off to the pigs now, can we? Unless you want to spend your golden years in a cell."

"Let her go, Haddon. I didn't sign up for kidnapping or murdering women and children."

"You signed up to do whatever was needed. But if you object, an extra body is no never mind to me."

Brynne had had enough. "Well, you'll excuse me if I have a slight objection."

She pulled the gun from her skirt pocket, but the material slowed her down. By the time she had her gun pointed at the thin man's head, his was pointed at Coraline's.

Brynne froze, the sight of a gun pressed to her baby's

head paralyzing her.

Taggart drew his gun but didn't seem able to decide where to point it. Instead, he aimed it somewhere near the middle, his eyes darting between the two of them.

Coraline whimpered in fear. The sound pierced Brynne's heart.

The hammer of a third gun cocked and Brynne's gaze quickly darted to the side, and registered another of Taggart's associates with his gun aimed at her head. The tall, thin man sneered at her. She ignored him and returned her attention to Coraline and Haddon.

"Drop it nice and easy, missus," Haddon instructed.

Brynne slowly bent down, lowering her gun to the ground. She laid it down gently and raised her hands to show they were empty. A slight movement over Haddon's shoulder caught her attention and she glanced into the darkness, taking her time standing back up. Richard stood with his gun trained on the thin man. His eyes darted to the side and Brynne's followed. Lucy materialized from behind a tree, her gun pointed at Taggart.

Unfortunately, the thin man caught sight of Lucy as well.

"She's not alone!" He aimed at Lucy and fired.

All hell broke loose.

When his associate fired at Lucy, Haddon swung his gun around to Lucy as well. Brynne reached for the knife at the small of her back. The second his attention was off her, she mouthed "Down!" to Coraline.

Coraline, her eyes wide in her pale little face, twisted in Haddon's grip and went limp.

Startled when his captive suddenly dropped from his grasp, Haddon swung his gun back toward Brynne. Her arm shot forward and she loosed her knife. With a sickening thunk, it buried itself deep in his chest. His mouth slowly dropped open, his eyes staring at the blade sticking from his ribcage.

Then he crumpled to the ground, his gun falling uselessly from his hand.

A gunshot went off over Brynne's head as she scrambled forward to gather her daughter. Another shot. Coraline wrapped her arms around her mother's neck and Brynne hunched over her, putting her body between her daughter and any harm that might come their way. Two more shots fired. Lucy shouted, her voice the only sound in the sudden silence.

Brynne kept Coraline's head tucked in her neck so she couldn't see the carnage that lay around them and crept to Richard's side. The thin man lay bleeding and silent on the ground. Richard stood over him, kicking his gun from his hand.

The hand that held his own gun trembled and his haunted eyes stared down at the man he'd killed. The first man he'd ever killed, Brynne was willing to bet. She reached over and took the gun from his hand. He released it, turning to her with an air of shock.

"Thank you for protecting us," Brynne whispered.

Richard's face cleared, his shock and horror replaced with such an expression of overwhelming love that Brynne's knees nearly buckled. He pulled them into his arms, kissed Brynne on the lips and Coraline on the forehead, and held them both tight. Coraline loosed her grip on Brynne and reached up to Richard. He took her in his arms and gently kissed her cheek.

Coraline wrapped her arms about his neck. "I knew you and Momma would come," she said, her voice barely audible.

Richard cleared his throat, which, Brynne had no doubt, was likely as clogged with unshed tears as her own. "There was never any doubt," he answered, hugging her tight.

Brynne searched for Lucy and saw her a short distance away, her gun still trained on Taggart. Taggart had his hands up, more as if he were fending off the torrent of words coming from Lucy than as if he was surrendering to her.

"Stay here," Brynne said, grabbing Richard's gun.

"Brynne…"

"I'll be fine. Besides, you need to start dealing with them," she said, jerking her head over her shoulder. Lamplights flashed in the distance and the murmur of voices floated to them. The gunshots must have been heard by someone who had naturally alerted the authorities. They would very shortly have a lot of explaining to do.

Brynne hurried toward Taggart and Lucy, who were locked in a passionate argument. Lucy glanced over, saw Brynne coming their way, and turned back to Taggart. A few more furious words, a lingering, regretful look on Taggart's part, and he lunged away, sprinting off as fast as his feet would carry him.

Brynne ran the rest of the distance to her sister. "Why did you let him go?"

"It wasn't his fault, Brynne."

Red-hot fury burned through Brynne, inflaming her cheeks with a literal heat she could feel pouring from her. "He took my daughter! He put us all through hell!"

Tears streamed down Lucy's face. "It would have been worse if he hadn't."

Brynne made a Herculean effort to contain her rage, but the events of the night had left her with little patience for Lucy's infatuated ramblings.

Lucy pressed on before Brynne could get another word out. "His associates were going to take her, ransom her to regain some of the losses they suffered at your hands. Finn couldn't talk them out of it. The best he could do was be the one who took her."

Brynne sputtered, so furious she couldn't force a coherent sentence past her lips.

"Think about it, Brynne. Please. Just stop and think.

Coraline knew Finn. She trusted him."

"Yes, which made it all the more easy for him to take her. He took her from me, Lucy! You aren't her mother so maybe you'll never understand the hell I've been in since the day she disappeared."

"I love her, too!"

"Then how can you defend him to me?"

"Because I know him. He never would have hurt her. He did what he did to protect her."

"That bastard—"

"Think about it. Was she harmed at all? Does she even seem frightened? How would she have been if one of the others had taken her? With him, she was safe. He took care of her, made sure she was well looked after. Would that have happened if one of the other men had taken her?"

Lucy had a point, but Brynne was not willing to forgive Taggart. "He could have come to us, told us what they were planning. Instead, he went through with their plan. What if something had gone wrong?"

"He didn't have a choice. They already questioned his loyalty. He didn't even know of the plot until it was already underway. That's why he left so abruptly. He needed to intercept them, be sure that he was the one who took Coraline. So he could keep her safe."

Lamplight flooded the area and shouts from the police filled the night. Brynne slipped her gun into her pocket. "We'll talk of this later."

She turned her back on Lucy and went to join Richard, who was trying to explain what he was doing in the middle of the night surrounded by dead bodies. The fact that he was a very respected member of society who was accompanied by two women, had a child clinging to his neck, and pointed out the false book full of money tucked firmly into the waistband of one of the deceased went a ways in his favor. When Brynne assured them she could produce the ransom notes, the officers agreed to accompany them back to the house for more questioning.

Brynne took Coraline back into her arms and sighed a deep breath of relief. She had her baby back again. The man she loved was by her side. Nothing else in the world mattered.

Chapter Twenty-Two

Brynne blinked in surprise at the visitors who stood at her front door.

"Well, are you going to let us in?" Cilla asked.

Brynne threw herself at her sister with a happy shriek that brought half the household running. The next several moments were filled with hugs and kisses and exclamations of surprise and delight as Brynne, Cilla, and Lucy were reunited. Cilla's husband Leo and Richard stood awkwardly nodding at one another and Coraline was on the floor already playing with her new cousin who toddled around the foyer, looking with interest at his surroundings.

Once the bedlam of their reunion had died down a bit, Brynne ushered them all into the parlor.

"What are you doing here?" Brynne asked.

"You didn't think I'd miss my big sister's wedding, did you?"

Brynne hugged her again. "I'm so glad you came. I never dreamed you'd be able to."

"Well, I also heard that Blood Blade had decided to visit the east coast. I reckoned maybe I'd better scurry my tail up here and find out what was going on."

Brynne frowned, wondering how Cilla could have known about her latest banditry activities.

"Lucy may have mentioned a nightly excursion or two in her letters," Cilla said, leveling Brynne with a pointed look. "Why didn't you send word you were in trouble?"

Brynne sighed. Her younger sister still thought Brynne needed looking after. But that was one of the things Brynne loved about her. Aggravating as it might be. "Because there was nothing you could do to help, and I had the situation under control."

"Really?" Cilla pulled out a newspaper clipping.

Brynne unfolded it, revealing the article that had been written after Coraline's kidnapping. "It was taken care of. Coraline is safe and sound."

Cilla's glance darted to Lucy. "And the elusive Mr. Taggart?"

Lucy's head jerked up, all joy from her sister's arrival fading. "I haven't heard from him."

Lucy stood and gathered Cilla's little boy in her arms and took Coraline by the hand. "I think I'll take the children to the kitchen for a treat."

Brynne watched them leave, her frown of concern lightening when she gazed at Cilla's son.

"He's precious, Cilla."

Cilla broke out in a proud grin. "Isn't he? You don't mind that we named him Jacob, do you?"

Brynne reached over and squeezed her sister's hand. "Not at all. I think Jake would be happy to have his nephew bear his name."

"Good. Well, now. Tell me what's really been going on."

Brynne filled her in on the past several months, from her decision to bring Blood Blade out of retirement to the showdown at the park the night they got Coraline back. Cilla listened, nodded, and cut right to the heart of the matter.

"Lucy is still pining for Taggart then?"

Brynne sighed. "Yes. It's been more than a month with no word, no sighting of him. I think she still holds out hope that he'll come back."

"And how would you feel about that?"

"I don't know. If you'd asked me before all this...I...don't know."

Cilla nodded. "Do you believe his version of the events?"

"Again, I don't know. It does make sense. And if I'd had to choose between Coraline being in his care or with one of the others..." Brynne shuddered. "Coraline came to no harm. She doesn't have nightmares, doesn't seem overly affected by the incident. So he must have shielded her well. For that, I am grateful. But, suffering through those days that she was missing..." Brynne sighed again.

"Well," Cilla said, leaning forward to grab her sister's hand. "Nothing we can do about any of that now. Let's focus on something a little more fun. We've got a wedding to prepare for."

Brynne flushed and glanced at Richard. He and Leo appeared to be getting on well, a fact for which Brynne was thankful considering the hullabaloo that had occurred when Richard had discovered Leo had been married to Brynne, even if it was in name only.

"At least we don't have to worry about this groom bolting," Cilla said with a wink.

That startled a laugh out of Brynne. "I hope not."

Richard met her gaze across the room. His smile warmed her inside and out. This time, her wedding would be real. And *legal*. She'd be walking down the aisle to stand beside the man she wanted to spend the rest of her life with. A small part of her still mourned for Jake, would always mourn for him. But Jake was her past. Richard was her present, her future.

And she couldn't wait to begin her life with him.

Epilogue

"Pardon me, Mrs. Oliver, but I found this in Miss Lucy's room," Mary said, holding out a folded note to Brynne.

"Thank you, Mary."

Brynne took the note and sat down, closing her eyes against a sudden wave of nausea. The bouts of illness with this baby were much worse than she'd had with Coraline and Brynne prayed it would abate soon. Hopefully, this little one wouldn't make as early an appearance as Coraline had or eyebrows would be set to waggling yet again. They'd only just found out for sure, but she'd had a good suspicion that she'd been expecting when she and Richard had said their vows a few weeks back.

Brynne read the paper she held in suddenly shaking hands. The blood rushed from her head so quickly she felt faint.

Richard caught sight of her from across the room and hurried to her side.

"What is it? What's wrong? Is it the child?"

Brynne's hand strayed to her belly, caressed the small

bump that hadn't yet begun to show. "No, I'm fine. The baby is fine. It's…it's Lucy."

She handed him the letter. His frown deepened as he read. Cilla joined them.

"What's wrong?"

Brynne slumped into the nearest chair. "Lucy is gone."

"What?"

"She's gone. She's gone off to find that betraying son of a bi—"

"I thought she'd gotten over all that nonsense," Cilla said, taking the letter from Richard.

"Apparently not," Brynne said.

"Well." Cilla turned to Leo who'd come up behind her to read the letter over her shoulder. "Looks like our visit has been extended."

Brynne's eyebrows shot up, but she nodded, grim determination filling her. "The children can stay with Cora. She'll be thrilled to get more time with her grandson and she's always asking for more time with Coraline."

Cilla shook her head. "Brynne, Leo and I can handle this. You shouldn't be traveling in your condition."

Brynne's eyes narrowed and Leo chuckled. Richard looked at him, his own eyebrow raised in question.

"A bit familiar is all. Better stand back and let them work it out."

Brynne ignored them, though she took a second to shoot them both a glare before she turned her attention back to her sister. "We are not going through this again, Cilla. I am perfectly capable of searching for Lucy and am doubly responsible for finding her. It's my fault. I'm the one that brought that man into our lives. If anyone is going to find them and put a stop to his meddling with our family, it's going to be me."

"You have to consider your child…"

"I did much more than travel when I was much farther along with Coraline and we were both perfectly fine."

"You were not, you almost died!"

"That wasn't because of my activities, and you know it. Besides, this is different. The conditions won't be nearly so bad—"

"You can't know that. They might be worse!"

Brynne headed for the door, Cilla following along behind.

"You always look for the worst in every situation," Brynne said, her voice getting farther away as she started up the stairs.

"I do not. I'm realistic enough to…." Their voices faded away.

Richard looked at Leo. "Should I be concerned?"

Leo laughed, not trying to hide his amusement now that the women were no longer within ear shot. "No. They'll get it sorted out. They always do."

"Well then. Seems like I have a few arrangements to make."

Leo nodded and clapped him on the shoulder. "Looks like the Blood Blade Sisters are riding again."

Acknowledgments

My deepest thanks to all those who have helped get this book out in the world. It truly takes a village and I have been blessed with an amazing support system.

To my husband and kids—Tom, Connor, Ryanna, Kyelie, and Matt—I love you all more than anything in the world. Your love and support mean more than I can say. To my family, the best cheerleading team in the world—Mike and Laurie Marquis, Ryan, Jeanette, Shaun, and Brandon Marquis, and to Mindy, Gail, and Michelle—my forever love. Thank you so much for everything.

To my amazing editors, Erin Molta and Gwen Hayes—thank you so much for all you do. You take so much of the stress out of this process. Thank you for pushing me to dig deeper and write better. It's so easy to get caught up in the deadlines and forget the craft, so thank you for keeping me on course and helping me write the best story I can. My books and I are in excellent hands! To my awesome publicist Renée Rosen, and to the rest of the incredible Entangled team—thank you! I so appreciate all the hard work you do.

To my writer buds—Toni Kerr, Kristal Shaff, Lisa Amowitz, Cole Gibsen, Christine Fonseca, Bethany Wiggins, Bonny Anderson, Robyn DeHart—for your support, friendship, and encouragement. Surviving without you would be near impossible. Thank you a million times over.

About the Author

Romance and non-fiction author Michelle McLean spent 98% of her formative years with her nose in a book indulging in her love of reading and research. Expanding that love into writing was inevitable. Michelle has a B.S. in History, a M.A. in English, and tends to be a bit of an organized mess with an insatiable love of books and more weird quirks than you can shake a stick at.

She is the author of the historical romances *To Trust a Thief* (Entangled Scandalous Jan., 2013), the *Blood Blade Sisters* trilogy (Entangled Scandalous 2013), a zombie fairy tale retelling *Wish Upon a Star* (Entangled Ever After Aug., 2013), and the non-fiction *Homework Helpers: Essays and Term Papers*. She is a contributor on The Naked Hero, and the Operation Awesome and Scene 13 blogs, as well as maintaining her personal blog.

If she's not editing, reading or chasing her kids around, she can usually be found in a quiet corner working on her next book. Michelle resides in PA with her husband and two young children, an insanely hyper dog, and two very spoiled cats. Visit Michelle's website: www.michellemcleanbooks.com.

Get Scandalous with these historical reads...

Real Earls Break the Rules
an *Infamous Somertons* novel by Tina Gabrielle

Brandon St. Clair, the Earl of Vale, has never been one to follow the rules. Even though he must marry a wealthy heiress so that he can be rid of the pile of debt he inherited with his title, he can't stop thinking of another. Amelia Somerton is the daughter of a forger and is *not* a suitable wife. But that doesn't stop Brandon from making Amelia a different offer, the kind that breaks every rule of etiquette... But what begins as a simple arrangement, soon escalates into much more, and as the heat between them sizzles, each encounter becomes a lesson in seduction.

Seducing the Marquess
a *Lords and Ladies in Love* novel by Callie Hutton

Richard, the Marquess of Devon is satisfied with his ton marriage. His wife of five months, Lady Eugenia Devon wants her very proper husband to fall in love with her. After finding a naughty book, she begins a campaign to change the rules. Her much changed and decidedly wicked behavior drives her husband to wonder if his perfect Lady has taken a lover. But the only man Eugenia wants is her husband. The book can bring sizzling desire to the marriage or cause an explosion.

To Win a Viscount
a *Daughters of Amhurst* novel by Frances Fowlkes

To gain a certain marquess's notice, Lady Albina Beauchamp aims to win the derby and asks a handsome groom to train her. Although groom Edmund White believes beautiful Lady Albina's notions of racing are ridiculous, her determination, pluck, and spirit have him not only agreeing to help, but asking for payment: each lesson for a kiss.

Made in the USA
Middletown, DE
18 November 2022

15418247R00137